Redeemed The Blood Of Jesus

The Life and Testimony of Dale E. Casas

Dale E. Casas

iUniverse, Inc.
New York Bloomington

Redeemed The Blood Of Jesus
The Life and Testimony of Dale E. Casas

iUniverse books may be ordered through booksellers or by contacting:

iUniverse
1663 Liberty Drive
Bloomington, IN 47403
www.iuniverse.com
1-800-Authors (1-800-288-4677)

ISBN: 978-1-4401-9227-2 (sc)
ISBN: 978-1-4401-9228-9 (ebk)

Printed in the United States of America

iUniverse rev. date: 11/9/2009

Introduction

The book Redeemed is about my life and how I was redeemed by the blood of Jesus. Jesus allowed Himself to be killed on the cross. His blood was shed as payment for every sin that every person has ever done and will do. When anyone confesses that they are a sinner and believes in the act of Jesus shedding his blood on the cross for their sins they can also have redemtion from their sins, be filled with the Holy Spirit and go to heaven to live for ever with Jesus. Those who don't confess that they are a sinner to God will surely go to hell. Hell does exist because I have seen it. It is real and I almost went there forever. Had I not of cried out to God and asked him to spare me from hell I would of been there now instead of writing this book. I received a very special blessing from God. He knew that I would believe in His Son Jesus and repent of my sins when I had heard the gospel preached to me. That is why Jesus intervened in my life the night I had the truck accident. Before the accident I had never had the gospel preached to me and had never been told that I was a sinner and needed Jesus in my heart. Because God knew that I would repent and believe He spared my life that night of the accident. He let me see Jesus face to face. I am no different from anyone else. What I do have is redemption in the blood of Jesus Christ and salvation. There is one other thing that I have and that is the Holy Spirit in my heart.

This bears witness to my spirit and soul that Jesus died and rose again. The more you seek God the more you will get. If you seek only a little you will get only a little.

People are so distracted by the things and cares of the world that they rarely even think about eternity. Most people don't stop to think what will happen the moment that they die. Where they will spend eternity is their choice. It can be spent in heaven or hell. Each person makes that choice. By confessing with your mouth to God that you are a sinner and believing that Jesus died for your sins and was raised on the third day you are exercising the measure of faith that God has given you. Then the Holy Spirit enters into your heart and you are filled with a new wisdom about God. You know that God is real and so is His Son Jesus.

I repented and went to a church and met a very special brother in the Lord, his name is Carey Fristrup. He took me under his wing and started discipleing me. He has continued this discipleship for more than twenty years. Discipleship is a very necessary part of being a productive servant of Jesus.

I have shared with many people the reality of Jesus and that God is real and we all need to repent and believe in Jesus Christ. Look around and focus on what you see. Everything that you see was made by God. It didn't just happen by accident. So many people take my words with less than a grain of salt. God has inspired me to write this book of my life and testimony of my experiences with Jesus. All of the experiences in this book are true and actual things that I have experienced. My experiences and testimonies have been written in hopes that they will open the eyes and hearts of all who don't know Jesus Christ as their personal Savior. I will never stop preaching salvation by the blood of Jesus Christ. What proof does anyone have that there is a way to have eternal life in paradise besides by the blood of Jesus.

Satan who is real and exist today spends all day everyday doing everything in his power to deceive people and keep them focused on feeding their flesh and pursuing their lustful desires so they will not stop to think about heaven and hell and that they will go to hell if they don't have salvation from Jesus.

Anyone that reaches out to Jesus Christ will encounter Him and the Holy Spirit. He is alive today. God knew me from the foundation of the universe. He knew that I would accept His Son Jesus as my Redeemer when I was told the fact that I was a sinner and needed to repent and believe in Jesus. God is using my life and experiences as a witness to help others to see the truth. The truth is that we are all sinners. Without a Savior (Jesus is the only One) nobody can go to heaven. They will go to hell. Your sins must be forgiven and Jesus is the only one that can forgive us for our sins. God is using my life and experiences to open the eyes and hearts of people to the reality of God, Jesus, and the Holy Spirit heaven and hell. Don't be deceived by satan and end up in hell. You have the free will and ability to believe in Jesus Christ.

Chapter 1 Live Oaks Springs

I was born on November 15, 1952 at the Brawley hospital. Brawley is 15 miles north of El Centro in California. El Centro is 120 east of San Diego and ten miles north of the Mexico border. El Centro is where I grew up. When I was young El Centro was a very small town. Everybody knew everyone else in town. My family lived in San Diego for about one year when I was two years old. I don't remember to much about that time as I was to small. Then we moved back to El Centro to 408 El Centro avenue. When I was four years I started kindergarden at Mc Kinley school. This was on Park Avenue which was very close to our house. My classroom was a very old building away from the main school. We didn't have air-conditioning then so it was very warm in the classroom in the months of May and June. There was a small room off of the main classroom where the teacher would send kids for a time out when they were misbehaving. I spent a lot of time in this room. About half way through the year we moved over to the newly built Mc Kinley school on north eighth street. This was about eight blocks away from my house. My mother would take me to school in the morning and pick me up after school as I was still in kindergarden. My best friend in kindergarden was a girl named Jeannie Carson. When I started the first grade at McKinley I would walk to school with my brother and sister. When I went home I would walk with a girl named Sylovnia Sager. She was a very good friend and lived on the same street as I did. Sylvonia would always invite me into her house for a drink and to say hello to her mother. Her mother was always so nice to me. Little did I know at that time her mother was a Christian.

Every Friday after school at McKinley there was a program in the auditorium called the nickel show. It cost a nickel to get in and they would show short movies and cartoons for about one hour. This was really great and we all looked forward to the nickel show each week. Simple things were so special when I was a small boy. We didn't have video games and Nintendos and all of the things that are available now. Kids made up things to play with and played simple games that were a lot of fun. Going to the school for open house was a big thing. Everybody went and people got to know other families and the teachers. There was a yo yo contest every year at school. This was a big deal to the kids.

My brother Steve is a year older and my sister Kathy is two years older than me. When we lived on El Centro avenue we had a two bedroom house. I shared a bedroom with my brother and sister. My brother and me had bunk beds and we were always fighting over who would sleep on the top bed. This was crazy because we were always falling out of the top bed because there wasn't a guard rail. We never got hurt but you got a big surprise when you hit the floor. I guess my brother and me were just like most brothers. We were always fighting and antagonizing each other. El Centro is a place where it is hot in the summer and cold in the winter. When we lived on El Centro avenue we didn't have air conditioning in our house. What we did have was thing called a swamp cooler. It helped some but we just tried to ignore the heat. We spent most of the time playing outside or sometimes we would walk over to the railroad tracks which were about a block away from our house. We would spend hours playing at the railroad tracks. The ice plant was next to the railroad tracks and we would climb up a ladder on the side of the ice plant and get on top of the building and get pigeon eggs and throw them off from the top of the building. This seemed like a lot of fun. My father had a pair of barbers clippers and every summer he would give my brother and myself a mohawk haircut. This is shaving all of your hair off except a narrow strip down the middle that was about three quarters of and inch long. My brother and me really liked this kind of haircut because it was different. Right before summer vacation when I was in the third grade at Desert Gardens

School I got my annual mohawk haircut two weeks before school was getting out. My teacher did not like my mohawk haircut and sent me to the principal's office and he sent me home with a note saying that I would have to cut my mohawk off before I could come back to school. I went home and was playing in the front yard at my house when my father came home from work. He asked me why I wasn't in school and I told him that I was kicked out because on my mohawk haircut. My father got really mad and went inside the house and called the principal on the phone. He wanted to know why I couldn't be in school with my mohawk haircut. The principle said he wouldn't allow it and that I couldn't return to school unless I got my hair cut different. My father then told the principle that I would just stay home for the last two weeks of school and that he was going to go to his office and punch him in the mouth. My father never did go to his office. I just stayed home the last two weeks and spent most of the days going to work with my father out in his farms.

My grandparents owned a cabin up in the mountains in a small resort named Live Oak Springs. This resort is about one hour away from El Centro. About 1957 when we were kids my mother started taking us up to Live Oak Springs to stay for the summer in the cabin because it was much cooler than El Centro in the summer. The cabin wasn't very fancy but it was great. The water for the resort and for all of the cabins and houses was from a well. The water was the best tasting water that I have ever tasted. The cabin had a wood burning stove for heat because it was cold in the mornings. We would make a fire in the stove every morning. My mother always made oven toast every morning. Live Oaks Springs was a great place to spend the summers. Saturday was always clothes washing day. This was a lot of fun because my grandparents had an old maytag ringer washer and we thought it was really neat to put the clothes through the ringer to take the water out of the clothes after they had been washed. We also made a ditch for the drain water to go down to a tree about fifty feet away as the washing machine was outside and didn't have a pipe to drain into. Some days we would roll tire down the hill over and over again, or catch horned toad lizards. One day we killed a rattle snake with a shovel. My sister, brother and myself all learned to swim in the swimming pool at Live Oak Springs. There was a general store at Live Oaks Springs called the Live Oaks General Store. They had the best selection of candy in the whole world or at least we thought so. We didn't have a television set but the Strom family had one. They had kids our age and we played with them often. So every Saturday morning we would go to their house and watch the Mickey Mouse Club Show. After watching Mickey Mouse my mother would give each of us kids twenty five cents to go to the general store and buy candy. In the 1950's twenty five cents was a lot of money and you could buy a bag full of candy at the Live Oaks Store. After we bought our candy we would sit on the steps out in front of the store and eat candy for hours. My grandparents cabin was right next to the Indian reservation and there was a house where Indians lived that was very close to our cabin. Every Saturday a lot of Indians would gather at this house and drink alcohol and get drunk. Then they would start fighting and hitting each other over the head with wine bottles. We would watch them and laugh. They were very crazy but they never bothered us. About a mile from our cabin on the Indian reservation was small pond. Sometimes we would go there and catch little frogs. The pond was always full of small frogs about one inch long. We called this place the frog pond. When we went there we always told our mother that we were going to the frog pond and she knew exactly where we would be. Sometimes we would go searching for these plants that had small air filled green pods on them. We called them puffer bellies but I don't think that was there real name. When you squeezed them with you fingers they would pop. We would do this for hours without getting bored. At the park at Live Oak Springs there was a round circle of cement about forty feet across. I think they used it for outdoor dances but we used it for roller skating and other games.

My father would come up to spend the weekends almost every week. There was a big lake on the Indian reservation and my father would take us there to fish. We always caught some fish. My father was good friends with the chief of the Indian Tribe. My father could go anywhere on the reservation and fish and hunt because he was good friends with the Indian Chief.

Every Wednesday and Saturday the bread man would drive his delivery panel truck through the streets of Live Oaks selling fresh bread. He also had salt water taffy and we would each get a piece. Sometimes my mom would buy a pie. There were a lot of other kids in Live Oaks that were there for the summer like us. Some of them were from El Center and some were from Holtville which is fifteen miles east of El Centro, We had got to be good friends with all of the other kids and their families. Spending the summers in the mountains at the cabin was an experience that most will never experience. We had so much fun playing without a television set, electronic games, bicycles. It was a special treat at night when my mother would make popcorn. On one side of the cabin there were lots of windows with screens. At night we would slide open the windows and the June bugs would land on the screens and try to get into the cabin because they were attracted to the light. When they landed we would thump them with our fingers and knock them off the screens.

Live Oaks Springs was a very unique place to spend the summers and I will always remember the special times that I had with my family there.

1958 most of the time in El Centro we were outside playing. Across the street from our house there was a vacant lot with a big eucalyptus tree. We built a tree house up in this tree. One day where we were playing at the tree house I was standing on the ground and my brother was up in the tree house. I don't remember why but we were taking some red bricks up to the tree house. As I was standing on the ground all of the sudden I was hit on the neck by a brick. My brother had dropped a brick from twenty five feet up by accident. I was knocked to the ground and dazed. God had to of been watching over me this day. I could of been hurt seriously or killed but wasn't.

In December of 1958 around Christmas time we rounded up some big cardboard boxes and some pieces of plywood and made a small house in the vacant lot across the street and decorated it with some Christmas decorations. Someone from the local newspaper was passing by and saw it and they took a picture of us kids and our Christmas playhouse and put the picture in the local paper. There was never a dull moment when we were small kids.

After Christmas in 1958 us kids started collecting Christmas trees after Christmas. When we had collected enough my father would take us and some neighbor kids out in the country with all of the dried

Christmas trees. We would have a big Bon fire and roast marshmallows. We did this for four or five years in a row. What fun this was.

Chapter 2 My Father

In the 1950's my father owned a gas station and a bulk fuel plant. He had a big fuel delivery truck. One day I was with my father when he was filling the tank on the delivery truck to go make deliveries. It had a big lid on top so you could fill it. I was up on top of the tank watching the tank being filled and fell into the gas tank. My father turned off the pump and pulled me out of the tank. I was soaked with gasoline. My father washed me off and I was all right. The could of been life threatening but again God was watching over me. My father would deliver gas, diesel, and oil to farmers out on there farms. I really liked going with him out to the farms. It was so much fun to go out into the countryside and see the sights.

One day my father had gone deer hunting up in the mountains by Kitchen creek with his friend Tom Kurupas. They didn't get a deer but my father shot and killed a big mountain lion. They brought it home for us to see. My father took it to a taxidermist to have it stuffed. Then he took it to the museum in San Diego and donated it to them.

I enjoyed going with my father when he was working. Some days I went to work with my father instead of going to school. This was more fun to me. The kind of childhood that I had was a very special one. As I look back on my life as a young boy I am amazed at all of the things that I went through. There were so many times that I had accidents and could of been killed. I can see now that God has always had his hands on my life. He would always protect me when I was close to death. What a special God we have. He loves us so much that

He will protect us so carefully. When God knows that a person will repent and confess that Jesus is Lord, God will protect that person until he repents.

In 1959 my father went to work for his godfather selling fertilizer and started farming. His godfather owned a fertilizer sales business and was a farmer. His name was Ned Moretti. He took my father in when he was in his teens. My father's real father was a very abusive to him so he left home when he was young. My dad got to know Ned Moretti when he was a teenager and was a jockey for race horses. My dad was a very good jockey and good with horses. Ned had a big ranch in El Centro on west main street where the Valley Plaza is now with a lot of race horses. My father used to ride Ned's race horses and was very successful. Ned owned a western clothing store in downtown El Centro named Tac and Togs. Ned saw to it that my brother and me had lots of western clothes and cowboy boots.

I was eleven years old when my parents passed away but the memories of my father and mother are etched in my mind. My father did so many things with us. Things that were very exciting. He taught us about the outdoors and the wilderness. How to hunt and fish. My mother was very special to me. She would always stay up late ironing the clothes and watching the Jack Par show on the television set. I would always stay up with her and keep her company because my father was always working late checking his irrigators or tractor drivers as they worked nights and days. My mother would usually go down to Maloof's deli to buy a pack of cigarettes before she started her ironing. I always went with her because she would buy me ten pieces of red licorice for a dime. I liked to stay up late at night but always got up in the morning for school. Being the baby of the family I got overlooked quite often. My parents were always helping my sister and brother with the things that they were involved with and I was always often overlooked.

Late one afternoon when we were returning from San Diego we could see a big fire in El Centro. My father drove as close as he could then we got out of the car and walked to seventh and Broadway. The Barbara Worth Hotel was on fire and burning. There were hundreds of people watching. The Barbara Worth Hotel was a very famous hotel and landmark in El Centro and the Imperial Valley. My sister took ballet lessons there in the basement. We watched for several hours as the hotel burned. The firefighters did what they could but they could not save the hotel. It was a total loss. This was etched in my mind forever. People talked about this fire for a long time and what a major loss that it was.

My fathers parents were very poor and Antonio my fathers's father didn't like my father associating with middle and upper class people. My grandfather was from Mexico where he was a farmer and had a big farm. But here in California he was very poor. One time when my father was still living at home Ned Moretti bought him a new suit of clothes so he could go to a special function at the high school. My grandfather didn't want him to go so he threw away the suit and told my father he wasn't good enough to go. My father was very much liked by everyone besides being a successful jockey and an accomplished boxer. My dad's mom was named Ruby. Her and my grandfather Antonio lived on a small little farm outside the town of Holtville. I didn't know them that well when I was young because my father didn't take us to see them very much. There house was very shabby as was their small ranch. My father was somewhat ashamed of his parents because of how they lived. I do know that my father would go to see my grandma Ruby often to give her money and things. In 1983 after I had asked Jesus into my heart I started going to visit my grandma Ruby. She was living in a small house in the town of Holtville. My grandfather Antonio had passed away years before. After visiting with her I would make a list of food and things that she needed then go to the store and buy them for her. She didn't have much money and God was blessing me financially so I could help her. Grandma Ruby was so much fun to visit. She was very poor but that didn't bother her one bit. She would tell me things about my dad and his three sisters when they were young. My dad had four sisters, Virginia, Mickey, Rosie, and Josefine. Rosie who I didn't know very well died of cancer around 1984. She had smoked three packs of cigarettes a day for many years. Rosie worked as a firefighter for a long time. Josefine did not like her name so everyone caller her Punky because she was small and skinny. When Punky was in her early twenties she worked in the fields and produce sheds for a living. I got to know my aunt Punky very well and my aunt Mickey. My Aunt Punky was a card dealer for many years and liked to play poker so she decided to build a bar and card room in Holtville. When she first opened up I would go over to her card room and play poker for the house. The house would front me playing money and I would split my winnings with my aunt Punky. I was successful at playing poker. I played poker for awhile to support myself when I wasn't working as an electrician. One day while I was visiting my grandma Ruby I was talking to her about God and going to heaven. I asked her if she was to die where did she think that she would go. She wasn't sure. So I shared with here about being born again in the blood of Jesus. I told her that if she confessed being a sinner and believed that Jesus died on the cross for her and rose on the third day that she would be saved and would go to heaven. So I led her through the sinners prayer and she asked Jesus into her heart that day. She passed away a few years later but I was so happy that she had asked Jesus into her heart. I know that she is in heaven with Jesus.

Chapter 3 Grandma Sones House

My mothers parents Harry and Eleanor Sones also lived in El Centro. They lived at 620 Sandalwood street. This was in an area where upper class people lived. My grandfather was very well off. He owned a lumberyard, hardware store, a plumbing business and an electrical contracting business. They had several air conditioners in their house and when we went there us kids would stand in front of them and get really cool. In 1959 my father started selling fertilizer for his godfather and farming. We moved out of our house on El Centro avenue and into a house at 417 Sandalwood Street. This house had central air conditioning, three bedrooms, and two bathrooms. Much more different than our house on El Centro avenue. This meant that my sister had her own bedroom and my brother and me shared a bedroom. This house was just two blocks down from my grandparents the Sones. This meant that we were able to go down to grandma and grandpa's house quite often.

Every Saturday my grandmother would bake cookies, bread and homemade applesauce. We went to her house almost every Saturday morning to eat these things. Then we would rake up the leaves in the front and back yards and get fifty cents each. Back then the city allowed people to burn leaves and trash in their yards. My grandfather had a brick fireplace in his back yard for burning leaves. We thought that burning the leaves was really exciting. My grandparent's house also had a basement. We would go down in the basement and play. This was really great fun. In the backyard was the garage and an extra room.

This room was the maids quarters but my grandparents didn't have a maid. This room was fun to play in also because my grandmother had all kinds of neat things stored in there. I was a lot of fun going to grandma's house. In 1960 I started going to Harding school. I was in the third grade. My teacher was Mrs. Christensen. The old school building which had wood floors where my classroom was is gone now and has been replaced with new buildings. Here I met a boy named Doug Harvey. His real father is Doug Harvey who was a professional baseball umpire. Doug live one block over from us on Lenrey street with his real mother Joan and his stepfather Wally Heard. Doug and I got to be best friends. I spent a lot of time at his house as it was close to mine. When we got our first report card from school Doug had got three F's. He didn't want his parents to see that he got three F's so he wanted to change them to A's after school. We went across the street from the school when class was out and hid behind some bushes and Doug changed his three F's to A's. It was kind of a sloppy job but not that bad. Doug's mother and stepfather found out that he had changed the grades and he was put on restriction and had to pull weeds all day on a Saturday. He told his mother that I was the one who changed the grades. His mother called my mother and told her what had happened. I told my mother that it was Doug's idea to change his grades and she believed me. Nothing happened to me. Doug's mother and my mother were good friends. They thought it was kind of comical but Doug's stepfather didn't. He's the one who put Doug on restriction. One year later Doug's family moved to the town of Brawley which is fifteen miles north of El Centro. I was sad to see Doug move away as we were best friends.

In 1961 when I was eight years old I started the fourth grade at Desert Gardens School. This was a new school. I went there for three years until I graduated. When I was in the fourth grade the Beetles came to the United States. I can remember this clearly because my mother bought us kids black Beetle wigs and we were the only ones at school that had them. They were very popular for a while. One day after school my brother and me were playing at a vacant lot on south fourth street when a car turned over. We went over to see what was going on. The man driving the car was laying next to the car and was dead. His head was smashed when the car rolled over. There were beer bottles all over the place. The police hadn't arrived yet so we were able to get up close and see the dead person. This was a very gruesome sight. I still remember this sight and can see it clearly in my mind even today.

My father got my brother started in baseball when he was nine years old. I started when I was ten. My brother and me were on the same little league team, the Newstars which was sponsored by the Newstar Market in El Centro. I wasn't as talented as my brother was at playing baseball but he was a year older than me.

I remember one time after our baseball team won the game my father took us to Foster Freeze to get ice cream treats. This was on Fourth street. I was standing by the curb watching the cars go by and eating my chocolate sundae. All of the sudden I saw a car going by and it hit something and ran right over it. I thought it was a big bag. Then the car hit a parked car and kept on going down the street. I looked back to see what it was that the car had run over because it was only a few feet away from where I was standing. After staring for a few seconds I walked over to get a closer look and saw that it was a man that had been run over by the car. The car had run right over the man and had killed him instantly. It was a very shocking experience for me. The driver of the car was drunk and hit about six more cars before coming to a stop in the parking lot of the 31 Flavors Ice Cream Shop several blocks down the street. I still to this day go to the same Foster Freeze with my wife and kids and I always remember that night when I was ten years old and the man was run over by the car right in front of my eyes. God has allowed me to see how fast death can come. It can come in the twinkle of an eye. No one knows when death will come to them. The question everyone must ask themselves is this. Will I go to heaven or will I go to hell when I die. Everyone will go to one or the other. Hell does exist as you will see later in this story. In a way my childhood was fun. We were always doing something and had some really neat things to play with. One day my father brought home a huge tractor tire inner tube. It was about six feet tall. We jumped on it and rolled each other in it up and down the street. We spent hours playing with this inner tube. The Mexico border is just fifteen minutes to the south and there was a very good Chinese food restaurant called the Shangri-La just on the other side of the border. We would go there to eat two or three times a month. Usually on Friday night.

There used to be a restaurant in El Centro called the Waikiki on Imperial avenue by Adams avenue. This was a drive-in where you could eat in your car or go inside. If you wanted to eat in your car then you would turn your heads lights on and off a few times until a car hop came out to your car to take your order. Car hops there were girls that wore grass skirts and had on roller skates. This place was really great. The hamburgers cost ten cents and were really good. They also had the best barbecued ribs. My parents took us to the Waikiki often. This was a very popular place for people to go. At our house on Sandalwood street we had a big dinning room table. My father sat at one end and my mother sat at the other end. My brother sat to the right of my father and I sat at his left.. My sister sat to my left. My father wanted my brother and me close at his sides because we were always fighting at the dinner table. From where he sat he could slap us on the side of the head when we would kick each other under the table.

My dad liked to go hunting and fishing a lot. We had a boat and spent a lot of time at the Salton Sea fishing and water skiing. Sometimes my father would come get me and my brother out of school just to go fishing. But that's not what he told the principal at school. We also had a jeep and would go out to the desert and camp out. My father had many pistols and rifles and always took them with us to target practice. Several times my father took us to Mexico to look for Indian pottery and arrowheads. We would camp out at night. Every year we would hunt doves and pheasants. We had a Golden Labrador retriever hunting dog named Mike. My father trained him to be a very good hunting dog. He was also very protective of us kids. I got a hunting license and a twenty gauge shotgun when I was eight years old. My father taught my brother and me how to use firearms when we were very young. We also had two motor bikes called tote goats. They didn't go very fast but were a lot of fun. My father used them to hunt deer when he went deer hunting in Utah and Colorado.

When I was about seven years old my father bought a ski boat. He was a member of a boat club and almost every Sunday for about a year we would go to the Rio Hardy River in Mexico to water ski. My dad always cooked carne asada, tortillas, and beans. This was very popular with everyone. My father sold this boat about a year later and bought a boat that was more for fishing but we could also use it to water ski. We started going to the Salton Sea to fish quite often as it was a great place to catch fish. The most popular fish and best eating was one called corvina. There were many marinas and cafes that sponsored fishing derbies each month to see who caught the biggest corvina fish. My father always had everyone in our family entered. Someone in my family was always a top winner each month. Occasionally my father would come and get my brother and me out of school so we could go to the Salton Sea to fish. I thought this was great because school was so boring to me. I had a very high IQ but no one understood it at this time. My father had all kinds of pistols, shotguns and rifles including a collection of old Winchester rifles. We went out often to shoot them. My father gave me a shotgun after my eighth birthday when I got my first hunting license.

In just a few years my father got to be an accomplished farmer. He was growing wheat, barley, sugar beets, cotton, and milo maise corn. This was being done on about two thousand acres of land. My brother and I spent a lot of time with my father out at his fields. Sometimes we would ride on the cotton picker or the tractors. This was fun learning about farming. One year at our house at 417 Sandalwood I planted some short rows of cotton seeds. I wanted to be a farmer just like my father. The plants grew and produced cotton balls. When I was ten years old I knew that I wanted to be a farmer just like my father. I knew all about the different kinds of tractors and the attachments that they used to prepare the ground for planting.

Chapter 4 The Vacation

My grandparents had been taking one of their grandchildren to Iowa every year on vacation. In July 1963 my grandfather took me to Iowa to spend two weeks on his brother's farm. We took the train back to Des Moine Iowa which is the capital of Iowa. My grandfather's brother Don Sones and his wife Berniece lived on a big farm outside of the city. They were my great aunt and great uncle. What a neat farm they had. My aunt raised laying hens for eggs to sell at the store. She also had three milk cows. They milked the cows by hand and I learned to do this one day. My aunt made her own butter from the cream that she got from the milk cows and sold the milk. She also had about ten peacocks. My aunt Berniece had a really big garden. She grew sweet corn, tomatoes, peas, green beans, cabbage, lettuce and a few other things. Everyday we went out to the garden to get fresh vegetables to eat with the daily meals. Vegetables taste so much better when they are fresh picked. Peas taste really great when you eat them right out of the pod. My uncle Don raised pigs and cattle to sell each year. I had some cousins that lived near my uncle Don. They were David and Patty Primm. There father Jiggs was my grandmother's brother. They lived on a farm also. I spent the night at there house. They had a really neat horse named Cindy and a big barn. In their barn was a rope that you could swing on from one side of the barn to the other and land in the soft hay. We spent hours swinging on the barn swing. One night we went to small country church that my aunt Berniece and uncle Don attended. There were about twelve people there. There was a man and a lady there that night preaching. I remember my grandfather saying afterwards that they were preaching fire and brimstone. We had been in Iowa for one week when late at night my uncle Don came up to where we were sleeping and woke up my grandfather. I woke up also. My uncle Don told my grandfather that there was phone call for him. My grandfather went down stairs and I went back to sleep. The next day when we were eating lunch my grandfather told me that we would be going home that day one week early because my father had been in a car accident and that he had been killed. I didn't really understand what had happened at that time. What he said about my father didn't register in my brain. We had planned to go fishing that day and I asked if we could still go for an hour or so. We did go fishing that day. Then late that afternoon we went to Des Moines and caught the train back to El Centro. It took about two and a half days for the trip. I guess I was in shock the whole time. I wasn't sure what had happened to my father. I didn't know if he was alive or dead. When I got back home my mother told me that my father was killed in a car accident. I was in a daze after that. Several days later we went to the funeral. It was a closed casket funeral because my father had been burned up in the car accident so I was told. This didn't help me at all. I couldn't see my father in the casket. I wasn't sure that he had died at all. I believed that my father was still alive and someone else was driving his car when it was in the accident. I would wake up at night and see someone's shadow in my bedroom. I thought that it was my father. One day I saw a car like my fathers car and the person driving it looked just like my father. I tried to run after the car to talk to the driver but the car went away. After that I thought that my father had abandoned us.

Life was very crazy after my father was gone. He was dead as far as I was concerned. I knew that I would not have a chance to learn how to be a farmer without my father. My mother didn't know anything about my father's farming operation. Her sister's husband Jim who worked in San Diego as an aerospace engineer said that he would quit his job and move to El Centro to manage the farming business. I know that he meant well but this didn't go well as he knew nothing about farming. Eight months after my father died my uncle came to our house at night to talk to my mother. I don't know what the conversation was about but I think that my sister does. Later that night when we were sleeping my mother committed suicide by shooting herself in the head with a 38 caliber pistol. My sister went into her bedroom first and found my mother dead in her bed. She told my brother and me that mom was dead. I was really devastated when my mother died. I thought that she just wanted to abandoned us and didn't want us anymore. I realized later in my life that this was not the case. My sister called my grandfather on the phone and he came at once as they just lived two blocks down the street. My sister, brother and myself went to live with my grandparents at their house. My grandparents thought that it would be best if us kids lived with my aunt and uncle. So we moved in with them. When I turned twelve years old my brother and me went down to the Social Security office and got our Social Security cards and work permits so we could work on our farm. My uncle bought two horses for us to ride. We built some corrals for them out in the country where we had six hundred acres of land. We would go horseback riding often.

Chapter 5　Moving On

I started going to Wilson Junior High School after Grammar School.
I started hanging out with a new group of people. They were Steve
and Mike who were twins. Roger , Jimmy , Pat and Johnny . I
started smoking cigarettes because my new friends were all smoking.
We would get together almost every night and hang out in the street.

After living with my aunt and uncle for several years my brother
and myself were not happy living with them. We decided to ask my
grandparents if we could live with them. They said yes so we moved to
their house. We liked living with our grandparents because they were
retired and gone a lot and on weekends. We were spending a lot of time
hanging out in the street with our friends but my grandparents didn't
know that we were really corrupting ourselves. In 1966 our farming
business was bankrupt. My uncle who was running it didn't know
what he was doing. He had tried growing high risk produce crops
instead of continuing what my father had grown each year. This was
mistake. We lost our multi-million dollar farming business after about
three years. Anyway my aunt and uncle moved back to San Diego and
my sister who was living with them went with them. My grandparents
moved back into their house on 620 Sandalwood where they had been
living when my mom committed suicide. My brother and myself were
still living with our grandparents. We liked living with them because
they always let us do whatever we wanted to do. Around 1966 my
brother started smoking marijuana. One day I asked him for some to
that I could try it. I liked it and started smoking it regularly.

One Friday night I had planned to go the football game at the High School with my friends. I met my friends at Roper's house. We were out in the back yard talking about what we were going to do. Then I asked them if anyone had ever smoked marijuana. They all said no. Then I asked them if they wanted to try some. They all said yes. I had brought three marijuana cigarettes and we smoked all of them. Everyone got high and liked it very much. After that we would smoke marijuana quite often. On the weekends we would get some beer and some marijuana and go out in the country and have a party. We did this with a group of girls that were in our grade.

My grandfather kept my fathers pick up truck parked at his house. He would drive it occasionally. He was saving it for my brother and me to drive when we got our drivers licenses. One night when my grandparents had gone out for the night I took the pick up truck out for a drive with two of my friends. I was only fifteen and didn't have a drivers license or driving permit. We drove out to a friends house outside of town. Sure enough a sheriff stopped me and when he found out I was only fifteen and didn't have a license, that was it I was in trouble. The sheriff took us home and grandfather went out and drove the truck home. He was very upset with me. Several years later my brother was driving my fathers truck at night. He had been taking drugs and wrecked the truck. In 1968 my brother got into some trouble. He got arrested for smuggling marijuana across the border from Mexico. My grandfather's good friend was the superior court judge and so he was able to keep my brother out of jail. My grandfather said that my brother would have to go away to private school. I was asked if I wanted to go to and I said yes. I was very close with my brother. So we went to Scotsdale Arizona to attend Judson Private School. My brother was going to be a senior and I was going to be in m junior year. Things went well for a few months until my brother got kicked out for using drugs. I stayed for the full year and got very good grades. But I was smoking marijuana and had tried LSD. After school was out I went back to El Centro for summer vacation. I was hanging out with my old friends all summer crusing main street and decided that I didn't want to return to private school. Going back to private school may have been a better way to go. But I was young and very hard headed and wanted to be around my old friends. My grandfather bought me a motorcycle when I started my senior year at Central Union High School in El Centro. I was spending a lot of time hanging out in the streets and smoking marijuana. Right after I turned seventeen In November of 1969 I stayed out the whole night without telling my grandparents where I was going. This didn't go over to well so my grandfather had me put in the Juvenile Hall Facility in the town of Imperial three miles north of El Centro. I was there for three months including Christmas time. After this I continued misbehaving. I was ditching school quite often and using drugs. To me school was very boring although I had a very high IQ And got very high scores on my SAT tests. The principal at the High School finally kick me out and sent me to continuation school.. This was a school where you only went for three hours a day. I went in the morning from eight thirty to eleven thirty. After school I went to my grandfathers electrical contracting shop for the rest of the day to work. By this time I had started using heroine. For Easter vacation I planned to Rosarito Beach in Mexico. I went with my brother and a friend named Billy. We were all heroine addicts so we stopped in Mexicali which is on the Mexico side of the border to buy some heroine. I was the last one to put heroine in my arm. The heroine that we had bought was China white and very pure. I had injected way too much and a few minutes later I went into a coma. I had overdosed. I would had died most likely except my brother and Billy started giving me mouth to mouth resuscitation and pounding on my chest. After twenty or thirty minutes I awoke from the coma. This was another life saving miracle from the Lord. In 1970 when I was working at my grandfathers shop I got caught stealing money from the cash register and was fired. I was a real mess. I would go down to Mexico almost every day which was only twenty minutes to the border and buy heroine and smuggle it back across the border. Being a heroine addict is a very crazy life. When your need to shoot up heroine you will do whatever it takes to get it into your blood as fast as you can. Myself and another friend went to Mexicali one night to buy heroine. We were hurting and needed to shoot up because we were addicts. After buying a gram of heroine we went with a guy who lived next door to our connection. We went out back to a small shack where he had a dirty bottle cap to cook up the heroine, and a dirty syringe to shoot up with. The glass of water that he had looked like dirty toilet water. We didn't care because all we wanted was to get the heroine in our veins. What is so amazing is the fact that I never once contracted any diseases from using a syringe and needle.

One day I was at home in my bedroom shooting up some heroine with friend named Danny. I injected too much and overdosed and went into a coma. My friend Danny started giving me mouth to mouth resuscitation and pounding on my chest. He was able to revive me after about fifteen minutes. If I had been alone I probably would have died. God saved me from death again. I don't care how many times you do something that will kill you. If God has plans for your life he will not let you die and go to hell when He knows that the person will repent of their sins and except Jesus when they hear the Gospel preached to them.

Chapter 6 The Military

I finally graduated from high school in 1970, a miracle. By this time I was a real mess so I decided to join the Army. My best friend Robert who also had a heroine problem decided to join also with me. We went to the U.S. Army induction center at Los Angeles and took the exam and were sent to Fort Ord California for boot camp. This lasted about eight weeks. During this time we were going through heroine withdrawals. As we were both addicted to heroine. Boot camp was not very much fun but I made it through all right. After basic training I went to clerk school at the same Army Base. After clerk school I was sent to finance school at Fort Ben Harrison in Indiana. This lasted about two months. I got a one week pass for Christmas vacation as did also my roommate. He was from Los Angeles so we decided to fly out to Los Angeles California together. We wanted to save money so we got stand by tickets. We were able to fly from Indianapolis, Indiana to Kansas City, Kansas without any problems. At the airport in Kansas City we were not able to get on any flights. Being Christmas Eve it was going to be impossible to get on a flight with stand by tickets. It was late at night and there was only one more flight to Los Angeles. We were hoping to get on this flight. The passengers loaded on the plane and the flight attendant said that the plane was full. We were very sad. A few minutes later another flight attendant came up to us and said not to leave. She knew that we were in the Military and had stand by tickets. After about five minutes the flight attendant returned and asked us for our tickets and said to follow her. She lead us onto the first class section of the airplane that was full. What was full was the coach section but the first class section was completely empty. As soon as we had sat down two people came in where we were. It was Elvis Presley and his manager. He came up to us and shook our hands and talked to us. We explained to him that we were stranded at the airport and were trying to get home for Christmas. Elvis was in the army also. The flight attendant had asked Elvis if it would be all right for us to fly with him in the first class section to Los Angeles. He said that we could. Elvis had reserved the whole first class section for himself. What an amazing experience this was. I got to meet Elvis Presly and fly with him to Los Angeles from Kansas City.

A week later I returned to Indiana to finish my training. After my training there I went to Fort Riley Kansas for two weeks of training to prepare me to go to Viet Nam. I had volunteered to go to Viet Nam but the Army decided to send me to Mannheim Germany to the First Maintenance Battalion. I stayed in Germany for one year. My first assignment there was working in the Clerk's office. This lasted for about two months. Then I was trained to drive big semi tractor trailer trucks. Three or four times a week I would drive to a different army depot to pick up a load of vehicle parts and supplies. I traveled all over Germany.

(Another miracle) One day I was sent to Kaiserslautern to pick up one thousand gallons of battery acid for the battery shop at my base. On the return trip back there is a very steep hill about four miles long. As I was going down this hill I lost all of my air pressure for the brakes. The truck started going very fast, more that ninety miles per hour and I couldn't use the brakes to slow down. At the bottom of the hill there is a curve to the right. The truck could of jackknifed or wrecked at the bottom of the hill but it didn't. I know that God had his hands on my truck that day. God would not let me die just yet because He had special plans for my life. After work there wasn't much to do so I started smoking hashish and drinking cognac everyday. Some weekends we would go into Mannheim to a place called the Atlantic Bar to party. After being in Germany for about four months I started taking LSD everyday along with smoking hashish and drinking cognac. One night I took some pills and drank a quart of whiskey. Soon after I went into a coma. My roommates took me to the hospital and the doctor there pumped my stomach out. I survived another drug and alcohol overdose. I was only eighteen years old at this time and a real mess. Soon after this overdose I decided to go to drug rehabilitation. I had to go to Ben Franklin Village military post to catch the bus to the Army Hospital in Heidlleberg.

At the bus stop there were two girls there waiting for the bus also. I could tell that they were Americans. They were about my age. One of them asked me where I was going so I told her to the Heildleberg hospital. Then she asked me why I was going there. I told her I was going for drug rehabilitation. When I got on the bus she asked to sit next to me. I said that would be all right. She asked me where I was from and I told he from southern California. She also wanted to know about my drug problem. Her name was Monica Angeletti. She was seventeen years old and a senior at the American High School. She was a cheerleader and her father was a sergeant in the Army. She had lived in Germany most of her life. We started seeing each other but I didn't stop using drugs. This eventually ruined our relationship. It was a miracle that I had a mind after all of this drug use and abuse. One day one of my friends asked me to go down to Augsberg so he could visit his sister who's husband was in the army. We went down to her house to spend the weekend. On Friday night after arriving we went to a bar that was only a block away from her house. As I entered the Bar called the Bonanza Bar I saw a guy sitting at a table. I immediately recognized him. This was Ricky Campbell from El Centro. We had known each other for many years as he lived very close to me. We had also used drugs together including heroine. This was amazing to meet him there. I didn't even know that he was in the army on in Germany. We spent the night partying. About one month before I came home from Germany I slowed down using drugs and alcohol. They had almost ruined me. I was discharged from the regular Army in 1972. My brother was getting married and I arrived three days before his wedding. My brother wanted me to be in his wedding so I was. I had to spend one year in the California National Guard after getting out of the Army. In the national guard I was the commanding officer's driver.

Chapter 7 Prison

Several weeks after getting out of the army my grandfather bought me a car. It was a 1968 Chevrolet Super Sport with a 396 motor. A month after getting out of the army I got a job selling car parts at H.& R. Pontiac in El Centro. This lasted for about four months. Then I got laid off. One day some friends of mine were going out to shoot their guns and wanted me to go. We went out to an area called the new river which is out in the country. It is a great place to shoot cans and bottles. I took my 44 magnum six shooter. This is a very high powered pistol. I had a belt and holster for it and was wearing it like a cowboy. I was practicing fast drawing and shooting at cans. There was only one problem with this. I had been drinking beer and was intoxicated. I went to draw my pistol and it went off in the holster. The bullet went out the bottom of the holster tore my pants and made a flesh wound along my leg to my knee. This could have been worse. I could have lost my leg because of the power of the pistol. God protected me from losing my leg this day.

I started looking for another job. I got hired at another car dealership selling auto parts. I met a guy who worked there and we got to be friends. He lived in Mexicali across the border in Mexico and came across the border everyday to work. He was a marijuana smuggler and dealer. One day he asked me if I wanted to buy some kilos of marijuana. I said yes. So a few days later I bought ten kilos of marijuana from him. I made a nice profit. Later on he said that I could start smuggling the marijuana myself and make more money. So

I did. Not to long after this I sold one hundred and twenty pounds of marijuana to some people who wanted to pay me with counterfeit money. I agreed to this because they paid me with five times the amount on money that the marijuana was worth. A few weeks later we were all arrested. I was charged with smuggling marijuana and possession of counterfeit money. I hired a lawyer for fifteen thousand dollars to handle my case. After eight months of court hearings I was sentenced to nine years in Federal Prison. My lawyer was able to get my sentence reduced to six months in prison and eight and a half years of probation. This really shocked me because I was only twenty years old and I was going to prison. In November of 1973 I went to Federal Prison. This was a prison camp that provided inmates to do work in the forest and to fight forest fires. My first week there we were sent to help fight a fire. At the prison camp the inmates do most of the work. There were inmates that worked in the kitchen. Some worked in the laundry. One inmate was the barber because he was a barber on the outside. Most of inmates worked in the forest and fought fires. Several weeks after I had been there I was interviewed by one of the guards. He wanted to know what I had done in the military. I told him that I had been a clerk. The inmate that was doing the clerical work at the camp was being released in few days and they needed to replace him. Since I had the right experience I took over his job as inmate clerk. I worked in the main office and had my own desk. Not only was I the inmate clerk I also inherited the job of running the camp store for the inmates.

Working in the office was special. I made eightyklllllllllllllll cents a day. The other inmates made sixty cents a day working. I also got to know the guards very well. One of the guards was Tony Amano. He was a real character. He liked me and the Juan Moreno the barber. On Saturdays when he had the day off Tony would come to the camp and take Juan and me out of the camp to go cut and split firewood. We liked this because we got to leave the camp for a few hours. Being in charge of the camp store meant that I had to go into town every week to buy things for the store. A guard named Bill Flores always took me. We were good friends. One day when were going to town in his car we drank a six pack of beer on the way to the store. After we did the shopping Bill took me to lunch for Mexican food. We drank two pitchers of beer with our food. By the time we got back to camp

I was a little drunk. Being in charge of buying things for the camp store I was able to buy special things that were not sold in the camp store when I went to town. Bill the guard who took me to town let me buy whatever I wanted in town except alcohol. We paid with a check from the camp store. No one else ever knew about what I was doing except the inmates. When we got back to camp from buying in town I put everything in the camp store that we had bought. Sunday was store day for the inmates. The ones who had special items that I had bought were charged out as cigarettes and sodas. They also paid me a fee for getting them special things. The inmate who ran the laundry Luis Reyna was a good friend of mine. I spent a lot of time down at the laundry. I had access to the storage room which was next to the laundry where all of the new clothes were stored. The inmate cooks wanted new white cook outfits every week. I told them that I would get them for them but they had to bring two cooked chickens, tortillas, onions, tomatoes, and chiles to the laundry every afternoon. This they did every day. They also had to supply me with coffee as I had a coffee maker in the laundry. Every Sunday was visiting day. Most of the inmates were Hispanic and they wanted to look really sharp for their wives and family. So I had another scam going. They could get new ironed shirts and pants for a price. A new shirt and pair of pants ironed cost three packs of cigarettes, a six pack of soda and two snickers bars. They would go to the camp store in the morning and charge the things that they wanted including what they needed to pay me for new prison clothes that were ironed. Every Sunday my bunk was piled high with sodas, cigarettes, and candy bars that I made from my special operations. I also made a lot of cash. When I was released form prison camp I had enough money to buy an airline ticket home and money to spend.

I spent Christmas in Prison camp. On Christmas eve the only guard that was on duty was Bill Flores. Inmate Juan Moreno had asked me to ask Bill if he would let him leave the camp for a few hours on Christmas eve to go with his wife. He said that it would be ok. Bill said that she had to bring a few bottles of liquor when she came to pick up Juan. I went down to the back gate with Juan when his wife came. She brought five bottles of liquor. Bill Flores the guard, myself and Luis Reyna the laundry supervisor got very drunk on Christmas eve at the prison camp. It was a very different experience being the leader of inmates at the prison camp. I controlled everything that went on with the inmates including punishment. I was released in March of 1974 from prison camp.

Getting arrested and convicted of a felony was one of the worst things that has ever happened to me. My lawyer had told me that he would get my felony record dismissed because I was under the age of twenty one when I was arrested. This was a big lie and he didn't ever get anything dismissed with my felony record. I paid this attorney alot of money and got very little for the 15 thousand dollars that I paid him.

Life wasn't easy after getting out of prison. I went back to El Centro to live. A few weeks later I went to work for my brother's father in law who was a cattle rancher. This was a hard job as I had to get up very early and worked until late in the afternoon. I moved in with a friend of my named Larry Bertussi who had a house. We were always partying every night with a lot of drinking. I wasn't getting much sleep at night and this caught up to me after awhile. One day I was late to work and my boss fired me. I didn't mind so much getting fired because the job was very hard with long hours and only paid minimum wage. A few weeks after this Larry's brother Giovanni stopped by to talk to him. He mentioned that he needed someone to work for him installing mobile homes. Larry said that I was looking for a job and was a good worker. So I got the job and started the next day. Installing mobile homes was a lot of fun. I was working with a guy name Tim. He was very smart about a lot of things. I learned a lot about installing mobile homes from Tim. Things went along well for about a year. Then one day my boss wanted to go pheasant hunting with me. I told him that I knew where a lot of pheasants were out in the country. He told me to take the company pick up truck home that night so I could pick him up in the morning and we would go hunting. This was on a Saturday. Saturday night I went to a party and was drinking alcohol and smoking some marijuana. About twelve o'clock at night I was on my way home which was outside of town about a half of a mile. I had just dropped off a friend Mark at his house in the town of Imperial. I was driving down La Brucherie road. It was about twelve thirty in the morning. The road was deserted. I veered off the road to the right and all of the sudden I lost control of the truck. I tried to correct it back to the left but over corrected and then the truck started flipping over and over in the air. I remember thinking to myself that I was in big trouble. What happened next was awesome. I was awake spiritually and I was traveling through the spirit world. I could see that I was traveling to this big black abyss that was hell. This scared me very much because at that moment I knew that I had died in the truck accident and was going to hell. Next I cried out and asked God to help me and save me from going to hell. Immediately there was a person hovering next to me. This person was special. He had on a white robe with a golden rope around it. His hair, mustache, and beard were white as snow. There were no shoes on his feet but his face, hands and feet were the color of shinny gold. This person spoke to me and said I was being saved from going to hell and spared from death that night. I would be saved from death and continue to live. I knew that this person that was with me was Jesus Christ. Next he disappeared then I woke up in my body and could see the stars in the sky. I didn't have a heart beat nor was I breathing. I knew that I had died and was very afraid. Then my heart started beating and I was breathing again. At that time I didn't understand what this night was all about. I would find out several years later.

I tried to stand up as I was laying face down in the dirt. I couldn't get up because my legs wouldn't move and I was in severe pain. I went into a coma after that. The truck that I had been driving had smashed and then sunk in an irrigation canal so no one could see it. No one saw the accident so I laid out in the dirt all night. The next day a jogger found me as he was running. He thought that I was a drunk person. What he didn't know was that I had been in an accident. He called the police and after they came out one of them saw the truck in the canal under the water. Then they knew that there had been an accident. An ambulance came and took me to the hospital There they examined me and took x-rays and discovered that I had a broken back, smashed spinal cord, a broken pelvis and my left hip was shattered into many pieces. I was also in a coma. Because of my broken back and smashed spinal cord I had been paralyzed. The doctors told my family that I was in very bad shape. They said that I would need many hours of surgery to repair the bone damage in my spine. Then the doctors said I would most likely die during the surgery because I was in such bad shape. They advised my family that I had no chance of surviving the surgery. My family said to go ahead and do it anyway.

Another Miracle! I made it through the surgery without dying. It was a miracle that I was alive because five or six doctors said that I would not live and would die on the operating table. It is by the grace of God that I survived. For the next two weeks I remained in a coma. The doctors didn't know if I would come out of it or not. Two weeks later I awoke from the coma. What another miracle. The doctors knew that my spinal cord had suffered a lot of damage and after I woke up from the coma they discovered that I was paralyzed from the middle of my back down to my toes. Doctor Kurland one of my surgeons said that I would never walk again and that I would have to use a wheel chair for the rest of my life.

Another miracle. Six weeks after being in the hospital my toes started to move and then a few days later my feet. Six months after leaving the hospital I was walking again. I had to use a walker for awhile and then a cane. At this time I didn't understand what was happening in my life. I went back to work setting up mobile homes eight months after the accident. I continued to drink alcohol and smoke marijuana and sometimes used heroine. I worked as a mobile home installer for about two years. In July of 1977 I joined the electricians union and started working as an apprentice electrician. My brother was already an electrician and they made good money. I started drinking a lot. After about two years I decided that I was tired of working for electrical contractors so I withdrew from the union. I went back to doing mobile home work. In 1980 I met a girl named Sandra. After a short time we started living together. We got married about four months later Her stepfather was a general contractor and was building some new houses so they helped us buy a new house. I got a job working at an electrical material wholesale house. After about three months we started selling marijuana to make extra money to help pay our bills and car payment because my job didn't pay very much. This was ok for awhile until I got arrested for possession of marijuana. I lost my job and things weren't going to well. My wife started hanging out at night clubs every night. One day she told me that she was going to leave and move to San Diego.

As I look back on this time of my life I can see that God permitted these things to happen because he was leading me into another aspect of his plan for me.

Chapter 8 Born Again

One day in January of 1982 I was driving to my grandmothers house. A friend of mine lived on the same street as my grandmother and as I was passing his house I decided to stop and say hello. God gets all of the credit for me stopping to see this person. It was a divine plan from God. It had been several years since I had seen this friend. I had been friends with this person in high school. His name was Sam. I knocked on the door and his wife answered. She said that Sam was home and to come in. I started talking with Sam and telling him about what was going on in my life. All of the bad things that had happened. Then he started telling me that he was a born again Christian and had asked Jesus into his heart about eighteen months before. Then he said to me face to face, you need to repent and ask Jesus into your heart. What he said sounded so sweet and true. His words cut right into my heart. I went right home and got on my knees and asked God to forgive me of my sins and to come into my life. I was born again that very day.

I then remembered the night of my truck accident when I died and met Jesus. Jesus had saved me from going to hell because he knew that I would repent and believe in Him that day after talking to Sam. At this time everything became crystal clear. Jesus spared my life the night of the truck accident because He knew that later on when I heard the truth about needing Jesus as my Lord and Savior because I was a sinner I would believe and repent and take up my cross and follow Jesus. This is why Jesus met me on my way to hell and stopped me. I was the one who caused the truck accident that killed me. God is the one who restored my life and did all of the miracles. The Bible has many stories about people that have been brought back to life. Lazarus, a little girl, and Jesus was raised on the third day. I died in the truck accident and Jesus brought me back from the dead. I bear witness to this. God gives life but more so He gives eternal life by the blood of His Son Jesus. Sam also invited me to come to church the next Sunday where he fellowshipped. On Sunday I went down to that church. When I went in I immediately felt the love of God there and the Holy Spirit. Two people there, Steve and Brenda Scaroni came up to me and gave me a hug and said we love you. I knew they did this because of the love of Jesus in their hearts. That day when the Pastor asked for those who wanted to commit their lives to Jesus in public to raise their hands. My hand went up immediately. After the service I was directed to go to a room in the back for some counseling. There I met a man and brother in the Lord named Carey Fristrup. He counseled me for a while. After that Carey took me under his wing and started discipling me in the ways of Jesus.

A few weeks later I came home after being gone all day and to my surprise the house was empty. Everything was gone except our Siamese cat named Moosie. My wife had taken everything but our one year old cat. That was fine with me because I really liked Moosie. She was my good companion. God took my wife out of my life because that was part of his perfect plan for my life. At this time I had a part time job that I didn't like very much. I was working as a salesman for Curtis industries. I traveled around to south western Arizona and the Imperial Valley where El Centro is. One day I had to go to a town called Tacna in Arizona. As I was getting onto the freeway in El Centro there was a person standing by the side of the road. I felt that God wanted me to stop and give this person a ride. This man had long hair and his clothes were very shabby. I stopped and rolled down the window and asked him if he wanted a ride to Yuma which is on the border of Arizona. He didn't say anything but nodded his head as to say yes. We had a one hour ride to Yuma. The person that I picked up didn't speak but only wrote on a piece of paper with a pencil. He told me a lot of great things about God. I was really blessed by this person. When we arrived at Yuma I stopped the car and asked my passenger if he was hungry. I told him that I had forty dollars and that I would give him half of what

I had. He shook his head as to say no then pointed up to heaven and smiled. Then he gave me a hug and got out of the car. I said good bye and started to drive away. A few seconds later I looked in the rear view mirror but didn't see him. I stopped the car and turned around to see where he was but there was no one there. There wasn't anywhere for him to go where I wouldn't be able to see him as it was an open area there. He just vanished. In the book of Hebrews chapter thirteen verse two it says don't forget to be kind to strangers, for some who have done this have entertained angels without realizing it. I believe this person was an angel sent by God to bless my life that day.

I decided to move to San Diego to see if I could get back together with my wife. After three months it was clear that she wasn't interested in Jesus nor being married. I eventually divorced my wife in 1984 because she had been in various adulterous affairs. I was so relieved when I got the final divorce papers. It was like a ton of bricks that were lifted off of my back.

I started reading the Bible everyday. I couldn't get enough of it. I had such a thirst for Jesus and what he had to say that some days I would read the Bible for twelve hours a day, day after day.

Carey Fristrup the person that was dicipleing me was opening a sandwich shop called the Brown Bag and asked me to do some electrical work for him. I did so. Then a little later on he asked me to go to work for him at the sandwich shop. This I did. I had a great time being around Carey. He was able to spend a lot of time discipleing me and teaching me. I worked at the sandwich shop for about one year. About this same time God called me to be baptized in water. A few months later I went to the men's Bible study at the church. Only three people showed up. They were Carey Fristrup, Mike Mc Cormick and myself. I asked Carey about the baptism of the Holy Spirit upon a person. We talked for awhile about this and then he asked me if I wanted to be baptized with the Holy Spirit upon me. I said yes. So Carey and Mike laid there hands upon me and prayed that I would receive the baptism of the Holy Spirit upon me. It happened at that moment. I was so filled with the Holy Spirit that I was drunk in the Spirit. Soon after God began to give me Spiritual gifts.

On day I went to the Colorado River water skiing with two Christians. Mark had a nice ski boat. We were there in the middle of the week so there wasn't anyone else there in the area where we were. After water skiing for several hours we stopped to take a break on a sand bar. We started talking about water baptism. The two brothers that I was with had never been baptized and were curious about it. I told them that I had been babtised in water and that it was a special time. They wanted me to baptize them at that time. So I explained to them the reason for water baptism. I proceeded to baptize them in the river. After I babtised them the Holy Spirit fell upon us in a mighty way. We became totally drunk in the Spirit and started singing praise songs. This lasted for several hours. We were all so blessed by the working of the Holy Spirit in our lives during this time at the river. It was the same as when I was baptized with the Holy Spirit upon me. It is my prayer that all born again Christians can experience this same kind of experience with the Holy Spirit.

God is so good to me. I didn't have a car at this time so Carey loaned me his VW to use because God had provided me with a job. This job was working as an electrician on a wind turbine project in north Palm Springs. After working on this project for about four weeks we were told that we would have to work on Saturday. We normally worked Monday thru Friday. We would be doing some electrical grounding on the 150 foot tall wind turbine that was being installed. As we were leaving Friday afternoon our foreman said that there had been a change of schedule and we would not have to come in on Saturday to work. The work that I was supposed to do on Saturday was underneath the wind turbine. On Saturday the wind was blowing about sixty miles per hour at the work site. The wind turbine fell over due to the high winds. It fell over and landed right where I would have been working. One of the engineers on the project was smashed by the wind turbine and killed. What a miracle this was for me. I probably would have been smashed and killed that Saturday. God was in total control of that situation.

Soon after I was able to buy a used car. I then started doing small electrical jobs. Then God provided me with a great used truck. About four months later I was able to buy a new truck. What a blessing that was.

One day a guy that I know named Brian hired me to come out to his house in the country and do some repairs. I went out to his house at about eight o'clock in the morning. As I was unloading my tools his wife Jodi who I knew also came out and asked me if I would like a cup of coffee. I said yes and went inside to get it. When I went inside and was drinking my cup of coffee I asked Jodi how her baby boy was. She said that he was sick and had a fever of 104 degrees. Then she said that her mother was coming out to pick her and the baby up and take them to the hospital. Immediately I was inspired by the Holy Spirit and said that God could heal her baby. I told her to get some olive oil and take me to the baby. We went to the baby's room and I put some olive oil on his forehead and put my hands on his head and prayed. I asked God to heal the child so he wouldn't be sick and also as a sign of God's power. Then I turned and looked at Jodi and these words came out of my mouth, It is done. I went right outside and started working. About five minutes later Jodi came outside with the baby in his stroller. He was happy and smiling. She said that he had made a bowel movement and then his temperature dropped from 104 degrees to normal. She also called her mother and told her what had happened. God performed a miracle on this baby that day. I witnessed this awesome miracle.

About six months went by and then one day I smoked some marijuana. This had a terrible effect on me. I chose to start using drugs again and turned away from God. Things went down hill after that my new truck was repossessed because I couldn't make the payments. I backslid away from the Lord for about two years. I was living in an old warehouse. I was being rebellious against God but he always provided for me.

Chapter 9 Shocked

In 1990 I called my sister Kathy one night and asked her if she would help me. I was having problems with depression. She said that she would. At this time I made a commitment to God that I would never use drugs again and haven't. I went to San Diego and checked in to a facility for people who have problems with depression. My cat Moosie stayed at my sister's house. I was diagnosed with bipolar disorder and they said it could be treated with medication. After spending two weeks at the treatment center. I was released. My sister Kathy picked me up and took me to her house. I stayed there for a few days. During this time I had a peace in my heart and felt that God was opening the door for me to live in San Diego. A few days later I went to look for an apartment. The manager was very understanding and rented me an apartment. My sister helped with the first months rent. I also had my cat Moosie with me. My sister helped me with kitchen needs and bought food for a month. She even bought me a television set. What a blessing. A week later I went to the electricians union office and signed up with them to get work as an electrician. As this was my trade. I got a weeks work right away. This gave me enough money for my next months rent with some left over. God was taking care of me and my cat. About two months later I went to work on a new hotel project. There I met another electrician who was a brother in the Lord. His name was Joe O'ferral. We became good friends. He was going to going to a church in San Diego so I started going there also. I had recommitted my life to Jesus. I was so happy that I had done this. One day when I was working at the hotel project with Joe I got electrocuted with three phase 480 volt electricity. I should have been killed by the electricity that went through my body. The electricity entered my right hand and went up my arm and across my heart and out my left arm. I was knocked silly for about thirty minutes. I was awake and could see the other electricians talking to me but I couldn't hear them nor could I talk. I was taken to the local hospital and checked over completely. The doctor said that I was all right but it was a miracle that I was alive. God saved me from death again that day.

In November 1991 my Honda car broke down on the way home from work. That night my sister call to see how I was doing. I told her about the car problems. She came over the next day and rented me a car. Then she said to go look for a new pick up truck to buy and that she would co-sign a loan for me as I had no credit at all and couldn't get a loan by myself. I found a new truck with a big discount on the price. God was taking such good care of me. My sister bought me a cassette player for my truck for a Christmas present. A few days later I was going down to have it installed. On the way to the stereo shop I was in a very bad accident on the freeway. It was not my fault. My neck and back were injured and my new truck was almost a total loss. This happened the first week of January 1991. Again God was watching over me and protected me as I could of been killed easily in this auto accident. I was off work for about eight months. Ten months after the accident I received $20,000.00 for my injuries in the accident. I invested the money in the stock market and turned $3,000.00 in a few months. I really enjoyed the stock market so I used my profits to go to a school to learn to be a stock broker to help me with stock market investing.

In 1992 I went back to work doing electrical work. Because I am a military veteran I started going to the VA hospital for treatment for my bi-polar disorder. They had prescribed for me to take 2,700 millagrams of lithium daily. So I was taking this amount every day. After about nine months I started feeling very ill. I went to see my personal doctor of many years in El Centro. I told him about the lithium that I was taking and he wanted to know how much I was taking every day. When I told him the amount of lithium that I was taking he said that it was way to much. He said that I needed to have a blood test immediately to check the level of lithium in my blood. The results showed that I had an extremely high amount of lithium my blood that almost killed me. Once again God saved me from death.

In August of 1994 I moved back to El Centro. I moved into a townhouse at 845 Vine Street next to the water tower. I started working for an electrical contractor in September. This was at the new Southwest high school. This lasted about six months. After this job I went to work for another contractor at the Sunflower elementary school. This project lasted about six months. Then I was unemployed for awhile.

Chapter 10 The jungle

In 1996 while at the dentist office my dentist shared with me that he had gone down to a small village in the jungle of Peru, South America with a group of Christians. There were several dentist and most of the others in the group were construction workers. They went to a village named San Jose. The dentist spent time there doing free dental work at the local clinic. The others did some building repairs at TEC Ministries the technical school in the village. The dentist told me that there was another group being formed to go down to San Jose, Peru again. This time the TEC Ministries needed to build a welding shop and a new classroom. They needed an electrician also. I contacted the leader of the group and told him that I was an electrician and was interested in going to Peru with their group. He said that they needed an electrician and that they would like for me to go. The cost for me to go would be $1,500.00. I didn't have any time to ask for sponsorship as I would be leaving for Peru in just over two weeks. I had enough money in my savings account to pay for the trip. I had such a peace about going to Peru. God had called me to go there. I went up to Los Angeles for an orientation and group meeting with the other people that were going to Peru. We got to know each other and shared the talents that each of us had. There were two dentist and a dental assistant, a pediatrician doctor, some general construction workers and myself and electrician. The dentists would be doing free dental work for the locals at the local clinic. The pediatrician would be seeing children from three local villages. In remote villages like San

Jose where I was going there aren't many opportunities for the local people to see a dentist or pediatrician. We had a great time getting to know each other at the orientation. We also found out that we would be going to a place called Pucallpa which was in the jungle. Pucallpa is where the airport is out in the jungle. This was a little scary as I had no idea what it would be like in the jungle or what to expect there. We actually would be staying at TEC Ministries in the village of San Jose which is about ten miles from Pucallpa. As I was driving back home I kept thinking about what it would be like staying in the jungle for two weeks and what the people would be like. Two weeks later I drove up to Hollywood to meet one of the missionaries that was going to Peru. I left my truck at his house and we went to the airport with some other people. We flew out of Los Angeles International airport nonstop to Lima, Peru. The flight was eight hours and thirty minutes long. We arrived in Lima about midnight. There was a bus waiting to take us to a safe house for the night. We finally got to bed about two in the morning. I woke up at six o'clock and took a shower with ice cold water as the water heater wasn't working. We had some free time before out flight out to Pucallpa in the jungle. We walked to a very popular market place called the Inca Wasi Market where vendors sold various handmade arts and crafts by the Peruvian artisans. At four o'clock we flew out of Lima to Pucallpa. This was a fifty five minute flight. The climate in Lima is just like San Diego, California cool and mild. There is a big difference in the climate in the jungle. It is very warm and very humid. Pucallpa is on the east side of the Andes mountains and in the rain forest. We arrived at the Pucallpa airport at about five o'clock. We were introduced to John Hocking who is a missionary and the administrator of TEC Ministries. From there we took a bus to TEC Ministries in the village of San Jose. This took about thirty minutes. Everybody was assigned a house and room to stay in. We awoke at six o'clock in the morning for our devotions in the Bible and then had a group prayer meeting. Next we had breakfast at the rain forest cafe on the grounds of TEC Ministries. This is where we ate our meals. Then we were introduced to the local Peruvians who worked at TED Ministries. We were then oriented on the work projects of welding shop and new classroom. Most of the people in our group helped with the construction project. All of the digging and trenching for the welding shop and classroom were done by hand. This took a lot of time. I spent about a week installing new fluorescent light fixtures in the carpentry shop and the computer lab. I was given two Peruvian girls and one guy as helpers. These young people were students at TEC Ministries. They were good workers but were more interested in me and where I was from.. I had a great time working with them and getting to know them. This was a real blessing as most of the old light fixtures weren't working and they had very little light in the carpentry shop and computer lab. They had been praying for an electrician to come down to TEC Ministries for a long time. Juan Manuel Vasquez who is the carpentry teacher had a paddle fan that someone had given him for their bedroom but he didn't know how to hook it up to the electricity. He asked me if I could connect it to the electricity and make it work. They had been waiting for three years for someone to make the fan work. I connected the paddle for Juan and he and his wife were so happy. God has blessed me with much wisdom about electricity.

One day John Hocking asked me if I could change out some old water pipes and replace a water valve that was old and leaking. I said sure. The pipes were for the water supply at TEC Ministries so I had to get it done as fast as possible. We only had enough new plastic pipe and fittings to do the job one time with no mistakes. I took out all of the old pipes and valves and put in the new pipes and valves. The glue for the plastic pipe needs about thirty minutes to dry sufficiently. After about twenty minutes John said that we had to turn on the water because people needed to use the rest rooms and other things that required water. I didn't think that the glue had had enough time to dry so I got on my knees and laid my hands on the new water pipe and prayed and asked God to dry the glue and bless my work. Then John turned on the water. There were no leaks and all of the work was just fine on the new pipes and valves. I thanked God for blessing the work that I had done.

The dentist, and pediatrician were busy every day eight hours a day. There are three other villages that are close to San Jose. People were coming from all of these villages to bring their children to see the dentist and pediatrician because of the free services. There was also free medicines. The dentist were very busy every day pulling teeth as so many children rarely could see a dentist.

I was introduce to Juan Manuel Vasquez the carpentry teacher my first day at TEC. He is a brother in the Lord. We became good friends. Juan Manuel is married to a girl named Irene. They have three children. Juan Carlos, Vanessa, and Danny. They have a house in San Jose but stay in a house at TEC Ministries. One Saturday after I had been at TEC for a week, Juan Manuel invited me to breakfast at his house the next day. I went to his house on Sunday to have breakfast with his family. After eating we were sitting and talking and I noticed that Juan's shoes were very old and worn. I knew that he didn't make very much money at his job. I had brought an extra pair of Reebok running shoes that were brand new. I asked Juan Manuel what his shoe size was. He told me size nine which is the same size as I am. God told me to go to my room and get the new pair of Reebok's and give them to Juan Manuel. I told Juan Manuel that I needed to go to my room and that I would be right back. My room was only a short distance away. I returned with the new Reebok shoes and handed them to Juan Manuel, and said here try these on and see how they fit. He tried them on and they were just perfect. Juan Manuel started to cry because he was so blessed to get the new shoes. I was so blessed because I had the shoes to give to him. God works in such wonderful ways. What a blessing it was to get to know Juan Manuel and his family on my first trip to Peru.

I only went into town one time my first trip to TEC Ministries. But I did spend a lot of time walking around the village of San Jose getting to know some of the people and the village itself. San Jose is a somewhat primitive place. There are no flush toilets except at TEC Ministries. Some people have wells for water and just recently the government put in a water system for those who want to pay one dollar a month for water. There is a primitive electric system there. Most of the people have electricity in there homes that is used for lighting only because they can't afford to pay much for electricity. The roads in San Jose are all dirt roads. Being in the rain forest it rains a lot. When it rains the roads become very muddy and almost impassable.

The village of San Jose is next to lake Yarinacocha which is very large. It is about one mile across at the widest point and eleven miles long. There are many different kinds of fish in the lake. They are very good to eat. Fishermen go out everyday and catch fish to sell in the market place. There are fish in the lake called peacock bass and they are the best fighting freshwater bass to catch and the best eating. One day John Hocking took some of us out in his boat to go bass fishing. We all caught peacock bass. This was the most fun that I have ever had catching fish. We caught about fifteen fish and took them back to TEC where the cook prepared them for our dinner that night. They were so tasty and everyone in our group got to try the fish.

There is a beer brewery just outside of Pucallpa. John Hocking knows the manager very well so he arranged for us to take a tour of the brewery. They make several kinds of beer and carbonated apple juice. After the tour we were treated to a feast fit for a king. They prepared beef, lamb and goat meat for us with all the trimmings. They also have a small zoo at the brewery with six different breeds of tigers. The brewery also owns about a dozen horses and we got to ride them. This was a very special treat going to the brewery.

One day we took a one hour boat ride up the lake to a village called San Francisco. This is a remote village inhabited mostly by Shipibo Indians. They make jewelry and pottery to sell in their village and in Pucallpa. The Shipibo Indians are very friendly and are very good artisans. Most of them speak Spanish and Shipibo.

We didn't complete the welding shop and classroom but did get a lot of the work done. Two more work teams followed us and the third team did finish the main structures. Only the electrical wiring was left undone. The night before I was to leave TEC Ministries I went down to the lake to pray. As I was praying and talking to the Lord I had a vision that I would come back to Peru to serve the Lord in some way.

Our work team was scheduled to visit the city of Cusco and the Inca ruins at Machu Picchu after we left TEC Ministries. We flew back to Lima and then flew on down to Cusco where we spent the night. Cusco is a beautiful city and I enjoyed visiting the Cathedral there and the market place. There is so much Peruvian culture in the Cusco area. The next day we went to see the ruins at Sacsaywaman, Tambomachay, Ollanataytambo, and Puka Pukara. These were some very beautiful places. When we were at Sacsaywaman I met two small boys who were selling some small ivory carvings. I bought one that was carving of an owl which are very popular in Peru. The boy told me that his uncle had done the carvings and that the ivory was from an old ivory quarry very close. The ruins in Peru are very amazing. Some of the stones are very large and have been cut and shaped to fit together. The Incas had some very skilled craftsmen and stone cutters. They also had some very intelligent architects. There are aqueducts still in use today that were built by the Incas and the Chimu tribes over fifteen hundred years ago. Later that evening we drove to a town called Urubanba where we spent the night at a five star hotel. We had dinner at a very popular restaurant there. The next day we boarded the train there and went to Aguas Calientes which is at the base of a mountain where Machu Picchu is. From Aguas Caliente we took a bus up the mountain to an elevation of twelve thousand feet to the Inca city of Machu Picchu. This is the most beautiful place in Peru. The city of Machu Picchu is still intact. All of the stones of all of the structures are still in place. Everything is just as it was when the Incas first built it. We spent the day there walking all around Machu Picchu. To me the Inca ruins are the most amazing structures in the world. There are about ten llamas that live at Machu Picchu. We had a buffet dinner at the restaurant there. The food was just great. That night we went back to Cusco to spend the night. We went out into the market place and bought gifts. Cusco is up in the mountains at about nine thousand feet in Southern Peru. Many of the people still wear their customary tribal wardrobe including the small girls up to the grandmothers. Peru has so much culture that has been carried over for years.

The next day we went to the Cusco airport and flew back to Lima. This is about a two hour flight. We stayed in the airport at Lima waiting for our flight to leave to Los Angeles. The return flight takes eight hours nonstop. When we arrived in Los Angeles I got a ride back to my truck in Hollywood from one of the group members. Then it was four hours and thirty minutes driving down to El Centro. I couldn't stop thinking about all of the things that God had done while I was in Peru. So many miracles.

It was so sad to see the absence of Jesus in the people of Peru. There are some born again Christians in Peru but not that many that have been dicipled. There are so many Peruvians that are hungry for Jesus and the word of God. There is such a huge need for spirit filled born again dicipled Christians in Peru be examples and teach the Peruvian people the ways of Jesus. God allowed me to see this need very clear.

Going to the jungle of Peru was so awesome. It is a very primitive place. Here in the United States we have so many modern things, and luxuries. So many people in Peru have very little and they live in primitive houses. Many of the houses have outdoor toilets and people take bathes with a bucket of water. Most people don't own a car either. Here in the United States almost every family has at least one car.

Chapter 11 The Second Return

I was a completely different person after returning to the United States. God had showed me so many things during my time in Peru. A few weeks after returning there was a reunion for all of the members in our group who went to Peru. We got together at the house of the Pediatrician Doctor. I don't remember her name but that doesn't matter. We had a really great time talking about the trip and exchanging pictures.

I was staying busy with some financial investments for the next few months but continued to think about Peru. Then one day I decided to call John Hocking at TEC Ministries. We talked for a while and then he asked me if I was interested in going back down to the jungle in Peru. I told him that I was basically free at the time and was on vacation from electrical work for awhile. He asked me if I wanted to come back down to Peru for two weeks and do some much needed electrical work at TEC Ministries. I didn't have to think about it for very long as I was longing to return to the jungle in Peru and missed the friends that I had made there.

I made arrangements with my neighbor to watch my apartment and take care of my cat Moosie. I called the airline and booked a flight from Los Angeles to Lima. A few weeks later I was on my way back to Peru. I arrived in Lima and went to stay at the Hinson house. This is a safe house where missionaries can stay for up to one month while waiting to go out to there mission town or village. There I met John Hocking. We had to stay in Lima for two days before going out to the jungle. A Peruvian friend of John Hocking's was getting married to and American missionary girl. We were invited to their wedding which was in Lima. It was a beautiful wedding. The next day John asked me if I wanted to go see some motocross races. I said yes because when I was younger I raced in motocross and desert races on motorcycles. John had a friend who was a Christian named Julio Chaing who was the South American motocross champion. We were going to watch him race that day. John introduced me to Julio and we had a great time talking and getting to know each other. We flew to Pucallpa the next day. It was really great to be back in the jungle. I went to see Juan Manuel Vasquez when I arrived at TEC. Juan and his family were doing just fine.

The welding shop that we had started to build my first trip was finished except for the electrical wiring and hanging the fluorescent light fixtures and connecting the electricity to them. I also had to install a circuit breaker box and bring new wiring from the main electrical room to the welding shop. This was a real challenge because I didn't have the normal types of material to use. As usual I prayed and asked God to give me wisdom so that I could get the job done. I was able to get all of the wiring done so everything worked just fine. God has given me the ability to improvise in such a amazing way. My two weeks at TEC went by very fast as I was busy working everyday. I did get to go fishing a few times and catch some peacock bass. What a blessing as I truly enjoy fishing for these fish.

One day as I was leaving my house at TEC one of the grounds keepers was looking at a papaya tree. It appeared to be dead as all of the leaves were brown and there was no sign of any green growth on it . The worker named Benigno told me that he was going to cut it down because it was dead. I told him that God could bring the tree back to life. So I laid my hands on the tree and prayed that God would restore life in the tree and that it would be a sign to the workers at TEC of God's power. The second trip I made more trips into the town of Pucallpa with John Hocking and got to know the town better. Pucallpa is the main city in the jungle and there are about one hundred and fifty thousand people that live in Pucallpa. One day when I had gone in to Pucallpa I stopped to get a soda from a street vender. I struck up a conversation with him. His name was Rafael and I told him that I was a missionary working in Peru. Then God opened the door for me to share the gospel of Jesus Christ with him. After several hours he prayed with me and accepted Jesus into his heart. I was so blessed. I found out a few days later that when Rafael went home that day he told his wife and children about his encounter with me and about how he had accepted Jesus in his heart. God has helped Rafael and his family so much since he asked Jesus in his heart. Pucallpa is a very unique place because it is so isolated out in the jungle. Everything has to be brought there by truck or boat by the river. The road that comes there from Lima the capitol is very rough and is only partially paved. It has to cross three mountain ranges to get to Pucallpa and takes about eighteen hours. Some things are shipped down the Ucayali river by barge. Almost everything that is sold in Pucallpa is transported in. Some fruits and vegetables are grown locally. There are many delicious fruits that are grown in the jungle. Some of the things that are grown are bananas, mangos, papayas, coconuts, cocoa beans, pineapples, guanabana, lemons, limes, and oranges. This trip I got to spend more time with Juan Manuel and was able to get to know him and his family much better. His mother and brother live in San Jose also. His brother Poncho is a Preacher. Juan Manuel has lived in San Jose all of his life. San Jose is a small village of about eight hundred people.

After spending two weeks in San Jose working it was time to go to Pucallpa and catch a flight back to Lima and then from Lima to Los Angeles. This trip went by very fast also. The two weeks seemed like two days.

When I arrived back in El Centro my cat Moosie was happy to see me and I was glad to see her. I enjoyed being in my air-conditioned apartment but I also missed the hot and humid jungle. I had bought some hand made spears and blow guns from the tribes out in the jungle and brought them back with me. It is hard to believe that people still hunt with spears, bows and arrows and blow guns. Buying these things helps the Indians with some needed income.

Chapter 12 The Taxi Ride

After returning from my second trip to Peru I couldn't stop thinking about the jungle and the country of Peru. I needed to focus on my work in the stock market so I started looking at a company that I had made money with a few years earlier. I decided to buy fifteen hundred shares of this company called Oak Industries. I wasn't interested in going back to work as an electrician just yet as I had enough money to hold me over for several years. My grandmother had passed away and left me some money. When I saw people that I knew I always told them about the trips to Peru. God was always the center of the conversations. God gives people different spiritual gifts. Some of the gifts that God has given me are the gift of evangelism, the gift of helps, and the gift of healing. God allowed me to use these gifts in Peru many times. For the next four months I thought about Peru everyday. John Hocking called me just to say hello and see how I was doing. He was in Tucson Arizona where he has a home when he is in the United States. We talked for awhile then he asked me if I would be interested in coming down to Peru for a month. He said that he had a lot of electrical work for me to do. I wasn't working at the time and I said that I could probably go. John was going to be leaving for Peru two weeks later so I booked passage on the same flight that he had from Houston, Texas to Lima, Peru. This was in 1997. I flew from Los Angeles to Houston and met John at the airport. After arriving in Lima we had some problems getting a flight out to Pucallpa in the jungle so we stayed in Lima for several days at the Hinson House again. The airline that we had reservations with made a mistake and so we had to wait three days to get a flight out to Pucallpa. One night John invited me out to eat Italian food. The restaurant was in downtown Lima. John borrowed a car from another missionary so we wouldn't have to go in a taxi. We parked in front of the restaurant and as I was getting out of the car a Peruvian woman who was probably twenty six years old, extremely beautiful and dressed like a bank president came up to me and asked me if I would like to go to her apartment. She spoke almost perfect English. I didn't realize what was going on with this woman. I was just starring at her then John grabbed me by the arm and pulled me away. I asked John what that was all about and who was that woman. He said that she was a prostitute and wanted me to go with her. I said that there was no way she was a prostitute because she looked like a bank president and was dressed accordingly. After awhile John convinced me that she was a prostitute even though she didn't look like one. I am naive in many ways and this encounter with the prostitute was proof of that. We had dinner and joked about what had happened to me.

The next day John called Julio Chaing to see what he was doing. He was free so we went out and picked him up and went to lunch. Julio is the motocross champion. I got to share with Julio about my motorcycle racing days and how I met the Lord.

Finally we got seats on a flight out to Pucallpa. The fifty five minute flight went by very fast. From the airport we went out to TEC Ministries. I would be sharing a house TEC with two other missionaries. Not long after arriving Benigno the groundskeeper came to get me. He had something very important to show me. We went to see the papaya tree that I had prayed for because it was dead. A miracle had taken place while I was in the United States. The papaya tree had come back to life and had green branches and six golf ball size papaya fruit on it. Benigno was grinning from ear to ear. He knew that the tree had been dead and now it was alive and bearing fruit. This was a real blessing for him and all of the workers at TEC to see God perform a miracle on the papaya tree. I was truly blessed myself. What an awesome blessing it is to be present and see God do miracles. I get goose bumps and wanted to run around saying praise God. Nothing on this earth compares to witnessing God perform a miracle.

The next morning I spent a few hours with John Hocking to see what projects he had for me to do. I would be doing some electrical repairs and working with some light fixtures. That afternoon I went to Pucallpa to buy some electrical material and supplies. The next few days I spent doing electrical work. On Friday there was a group of people that were coming from another village by boat to stay in San Jose. These people were brothers and sisters in the Lord from the village of Esperanza. They were going to stay at the church property in San Jose. This village is about two hours down the lake by boat. There would be about twenty six people in all. Some of them were children. On there way to San Jose there boat motor broke down and they got their boat towed to San Jose. After they arrived I went down to the church to meet me these people and get to know them. I started talking the person who drives the boat and takes care of the motor. He told me that the motor was bad and needed to be rebuilt. The motor was a sixteen horse power Briggs & Stratten motor which was very popular in that area for boats. Their motor was a very old model. His church was a very poor church from a poor village. They only had enough gas to make it to San Jose let alone money to fix the motor. These people were a little depressed when they found out that their boat motor needed major repairs. This boat was their only means of transportation back to their village. Our church in San Jose would be providing all of their meals while they were there as they were our guest. After I talked to the brother who was in charge of the boat and found out what was needed we prayed. Then God spoke to me and said that He wanted me to buy all of the parts that they needed to fix the motor. How amazing this was because I had taken some extra money with me for this trip. God had this problem all planned out. When I told the people that God was providing the money to repair the motor they were so blessed. The next day we went into Pucallpa to look for the new parts that we needed. After two days of searching and going to eight or ten different stores we finally got everything that we needed. It was a miracle that we could find all of the parts for the motor because it was a very old model. With only a few primitive tools we took the motor apart and put in the new parts and then put the motor back together again. I laid my hands on the motor and prayed for God to bless the work. The motor started right up and worked just perfect. The people were able to return to their village in their boat. God is awesome. God used me to bless these people and in so doing I got blessed beyond measure. There were only two people from the village of Esperanza that had Bibles. I had brought down two cases of Spanish Bibles with me. So on Sunday at church before the people went back to Esperanza I gave all of the families from Esperanza a new Bible. Their faces lit up like the sun. Bibles are costly in Peru and so many people can't afford them.

After work one day I was going to Pucallpa to buy some fruit and sodas. I waited for a taxi on the main road in San Jose. This is where the taxi drivers pass by. I got into the front seat but the driver was waiting for more passengers. They always get five passengers and maybe a child or two. Some people got into the back seat and the driver started off. I was curious to see who was in the back seat I turned around to look. There was an older man and a woman and a young lady. As I looked at the young lady she smiled. I asked her if she lived in San Jose and she said yes. Then I asked her what her name was. She said Gina Panduro. She lived right by where I had got into the taxi. She was going to her mother's house in Yarina which was on the way to Pucallpa. The ride to Yarina takes about seven minutes. We talked on the way to Yarina. Gina told me that she was studying to be a nurse. She said that the next day which was Saturday that there was a parade in Yarina and she would be marching in the parade with her class from the nursing school. I was invited to come and watch.

The next morning I got up and went to Yarina to watch the parade. Gina introduced me to Zaida her mother, Iris and Villa her sisters. I also met her brother Jimmy, and her grandparents Felix and Mercedes Panduro. I really enjoyed meeting Gina's family. They were very different because there lives and culture were totally different from my life. Gina's grandparents live in San Jose. Gina was living with her grandparents at the time. Most of Peru is very primitive. I am from California which is a very modern state in the United States. Gina had a one year old baby boy when I met her. His name was Marcos. Gina and her family attend the Christian Evangelical Church of San Jose. This is the same church where I attended when I was in San Jose. I didn't remember seeing Gina at church but she says that she remembers seeing me. I assumed that Gina was a Christian because she went to church. I didn't ask the Lord to prove to me that Gina was a born again Spirit filled believer. This was a terrible mistake. The next two weeks were very interesting. I took Gina to town every other day to eat chicken at a really great restaurant. They had the best broasted chicken and french fries. This was the best chicken restaurant in Pucallpa. We got to know the owner and his wife because we were there so often. My stay in San Jose went by very fast as always. Then it was time to return to California. Back at home in El Centro I thought about Gina alot. I called her on the telephone and we talked about me returning to Peru to live in San Jose. A few weeks later I returned to Peru to serve the Lord as a missionary. About six months later we decided to get married. We were married at the courthouse in Yarina. Then we had a church wedding at Gina's grandparents house with all of her family and some American missionaries. After the wedding we went to Pucallpa to spend the night at the best hotel in town. Then we flew to Lima and stayed in a hotel there for three days. We went shopping for some clothes one day to buy some clothes for Gina. I paid for the things with a visa credit card. Gina asked me why I didn't have to give the cashier any money for the clothes. I told her I was using my visa card and didn't have to pay with cash. I used my credit card many times while we were on our honeymoon. Gina got the idea that I could just get anything that I wanted by just giving the stores my visa card. She had never seen anyone use a credit card. One day she asked if I would go get a new car because all I had to do was show them my plastic card and I could get anything that I wanted. So I finally realized that she didn't understand what a credit card was all about. I explained how a credit card worked and that eventually you had to pay for what you had bought with the credit card. Here in the United States we have so much. So many people here are to lazy to work so they get on welfare and let the government support them. There is always a job available of some sorts. In third would countries people have very little. What little money they dofv earn goes to buy food first. I have found that the people in Peru are more open and willing to listen to someone preach the Gospel of Jesus Christ than in the United States. People here in America are so caught up in their lives with all the money and things that they have that they can't see that they really need forgiveness of their sins so they can go to heaven when they die. A few weeks later we went back to the courthouse in Yarina to get a copy of our marriage certificate. They said that we would have to go through the whole process again to get married because they said my documents weren't in order. So we went to Pucallpa and filed a new application to get married. The clerk said that we would have to wait about thirty days for the application to be processed. This sounded crazy to me. I asked the clerk who was the person that would prepare and process the application. He said that he was the person that would be doing it. I then asked him how I could get it done in one day. He said that he could process the application in one day if I wanted to pay him a thirty dollar tip. I said that I would pay him the thirty dollar tip and the next day the application was processed. We were married at the Pucallpa courthouse. This was our third wedding ceremony.

Peru is a country where everyone wants to make a buck because wages are very low. One day when I was in Lima I had to go to a bank to get a form so I could get a visa for Gina and Macros. The policeman at the front door of the bank made me pay him a tip just to go inside and get a form. This was because I was an American. I also had to get a police report for Gina to give to the American Embassy so they could see whether or not she had a police record. Of course she didn't. To get the police report we had to go the main police station in Lima. I talked to a police officer there about what we needed. He said that it would take thirty to forty days to get the report and that it would cost about thirty dollars. I then asked why it would take so long because we were on a time schedule with the American Embassy to apply for Gina and Marco's visas. The officer told me if I wanted the report in two days I could get it in but it would cost me three hundred dollars. I was furious at this person for trying to take advantage of us because I was an American. I prayed and asked God for help. I demanded to see his supervisor and was granted permission to see the police chief. I explained to him what had taken place with the officer who wanted to charge me three hundred dollars for a simple report. I explained to him that I was a missionary working in Peru and was marrying a Peruvian woman. The police chief said that he was sorry that I had been mistreated and that I could come back in two days and get the report that we needed and that it would only cost seven dollars. God intervened for me with the police chief and helped us get the report for the price that it was supposed to be and in just two days.

Chapter 12 Living In Lima

After our honeymoon we rented a house in San Jose. It was a big house with an indoor toilet and running water. We lived there for about two months. Then we moved into a house next door to Gina's mother's house in the village of Yarina. We were there for about three months. I came up to the states for two weeks. When I returned to Peru I met Gina and Marcos in Lima and we stayed with her aunt Myra for a few days. Myra was the administrator for a home for elderly Christians. After being with Gina's aunt for a few days we flew to a town called Piura. A company that I own stock in was building some homes there and they wanted me to go there and do some work on the model homes. We spent five days in Piura. The climate there is just like the Imperial Valley. Hot in the summer and cold in the winter. We had a great time while we were in Piura.

We returned to Lima and Gina and Marcos traveled to Pucallpa to visit with her mother while I stayed in Lima to look for an apartment for us to live in. We needed to apply for visas for Gina and Marcos at the American Embassy in Lima so it was more accommodating for us to live in Lima during the time that we needed to go through the process of getting visas for them. I went to stay at the Hinson House for missionaries while I looked for an apartment. I started praying that God would provide an apartment for us to rent. I only had three days to stay at the Hinson House so I was needing a miracle from God in providing a place for us to live. The first two days I looked at dozens of places but I didn't have a peace about them. Then on the third day I went to look at a place in the district of Pueblo Libre. This apartment was just right and close to a market place. The owner of the apartment complex rented me the apartment that afternoon. It was also close to where Gina's aunt lived. What a blessing that God provided this place for us. We bought a television set, a table and chairs, kitchen necessities including a small gas stove. We also bought a small refrigerator and a bed. Gina's aunt and her son Saulo came over almost everyday for dinner. There was an open air market about three blocks away form our apartment including a laundry. The market place was really great. They always had fresh meat, fruit and vegetables. The avocados that grow in Peru are huge and very tasty and inexpensive. We didn't have a car but there are taxis everywhere that are so inexpensive. It only cost about thirty cents to go to the market place. I had brought a laptop computer with me and we had a phone line in our apartment so we were able to get on the internet. The system was a little primitive and didn't always work but it was adequate. One night I was returning home from the store. It was about nine o'clock at night and I was about a half block away from our apartment. There was a group of young teens playing soccer in the street. I recognized a few of them from our neighborhood. A guy started walking up to me and at first I didn't recognize him. When he got right up to me I realized that it was the guy who lived above us. He said hello and asked what I was doing out at this time of night. I told him that I had gone to the store. He said that it was dangerous for me to be out late at night. I told him that I was not afraid and God would protect me. Then the rest of the guys that were playing soccer came over to where we were. They wanted to know who I was and what I was doing living in their neighborhood. I told them that I was a missionary and was living in Lima for a while. Then one of them noticed my tattoos and asked me about them. I explained to them That I had got them when I was younger and was a worldly person that was a drug dealer and user. They wanted to know more about me so I proceeded to share my testimony with them. I started with the truck accident when I got killed and met Jesus. Then I told them all about my life using drugs and dealing drugs and how I was arrested and sent to prison.

These young men that I was talking to were all gang members of a gang from our neighborhood. Some of them had knives and others had guns. The guy who lived above me had an uzi machine gun. I talked to these young men for about two hours. One of them asked if he could come over and study the Bible with me. He said that his grandmother had a Bible and that he could borrow it from her. Them another guy asked if he could come also. Several days later two of the gang members came by and I taught them the scriptures. They were very interested in Jesus and the Bible. God opened the door for me to witness to my neighbor and his wife who lived above us. We never had any problems when we lived in this apartment. The gang members said that they wouldn't let anyone bother us. I know that God was protecting us all the time that we were in that neighborhood.

When you apply for visas the American Embassy requires that the individuals requesting a visa have to have an exam by a doctor. The American Embassy sent us to a doctor in Lima. The examinations went well with a good report for Gina and Marcos. We returned to the American Embassy for our first appointment with an immigration agent. His name was Garry Fuller. He was very helpful at our first visit and told me to call him if we had any questions. Actually Gary coached us through the whole process. He gave us help that nobody else would normally get. He helped speed our applications through. After two months we were told to come to the American Embassy and pick up Gina's and Marco's visas. We were so happy because God helped us to get their visas so quick and easy. A few weeks later we made airplane reservations to fly to the United States. We were told at the America Embassy that we would be able to get Gina's and Marco's residency cards in two months when we arrived in the United States. We needed to get their United States residency cards because it was required by the Immigration department. Then Gina and Marcos could travel away from the United States and return any time. Then we could return to Peru. After being in Lima for four months and working on the applications for Gina's and Marco's visas the American Embassy issued their visas.

Chapter 13 The Long Wait

We arrived at the Los Angeles International airport at eight o'clock in the morning. It took about twenty minutes for us to clear through customs because of the new visas that Gina and Marcos had. After customs we went to Hertz to rent a car. From there we had a four hour drive to El Centro to the townhouse where I had been living for four years. Gina was amazed with California. It was so modern and different than the village where she grew up. She got a big surprise a few months later when it turned from winter to summer. The summers in El Centro are very hot. Some days it gets up to one hundred and twenty degrees. We have air-conditioning which is great when you are inside. The winters are just the opposite. It is very cold in the winter. In the rain forest where Gina is from it is hot and humid in the summer and warm and humid in the winter. During the rainy season it rains like cats and dogs almost everyday. Gina had to get used to living in the United States. One day when we were in the kitchen I put some garbage down the sink then turned on the garbage disposal. Gina had never seen one before. In the home where Gina grew up they did not have hot water. She was used to bathing in cold water and washing clothes by hand. We have a washer and dryer in our patio. We have an electric stove also. In the jungle most homes have a small two burner gas stove and use small propane gas tanks that have to be changed regularly.

When we applied for Gina and Marco's residency cards we got a big shock. The people at the immigration office told us that we would have to wait six months before they would get them. Then I asked if they could return to Peru because I was a missionary and we were going to return to live there. They said that they could only leave the country for two weeks at a time and then had to come back to the United States. We were shocked but there was nothing that we could do. After six months there were no residency cards in the mail. So I called the immigration office to see what the problem was. They said that whoever it was that told us it would only take six months was wrong. Then we were told that it could take two years before we got their residency cards. After waiting two years we were told that Gina's residency card had been lost and that we would have to reapply for their residency cards. We made an appointment at the immigration office in San Diego which was a real nightmare just to get an appointment. When we went to the immigration office it was so full of people and we were told that we would have to make another appointment and come back another day. I was almost depressed because it was a four hour round trip to San Diego and we had been waiting so long to get Gina and Marco's residency cards. I started praying and asking God to help us. Then I was told to go to a desk and ask for a new appointment. When I started talking to the lady at the desk I explained to her what had happened to Gina's residency card and all of the problems that we had encountered. I told her that we were supposed to have an appointment with a Mrs. Moreno. Then she replied that she was Mrs. Moreno and that they were having a very rough day with more that the usual amount of applicants. She said that she would help us fill out the forms and get in the new applications that day. What a blessings that God put us together with this person so we could get the help that we needed. We got the paperwork done and the lady helping us said that we would not have to pay a new application fee because it was not our fault that Gina's and Marco's residency cards had been lost.

We got everything done that day at the immigration office. It had been over two years now that we had been waiting for the residency cards. We were told that it could take up to five years before we got their permanent residency cards. This was not at all like what we were told in the beginning when we first applied for their visas in Lima. This just goes to show you that you can't always believe what someone tells you even the government. We would just have to wait to return to Peru to live until we got their residency cards. In 1998 our church here in El Centro started building a new church on ten acres of land that we bought. At this time we were expecting to return to Peru at any day. We needed to install some underground electrical pipes for the electrical service for the church so I volunteered to do it. I spent most of that summer putting in about fifteen hundred feet of plastic pipe in the ground. We were expecting to leave for Peru any day but that didn't happen. Gina wanted to go to Peru to visit so her and Marcos went down for two weeks. Gina was pregnant at this time with our daughter Martelle. They took several duffle bags full of used clothes to give out. Then about six months later as we still didn't have Gina's residency card but we planned a trip to Peru for two weeks. The immigration allowed Gina and Marcos to leave the country for short periods of time but not for a long time. At this time I was working out of town in the city of Carlsbad which is north of San Diego. I was staying at my sisters house during the week and driving home every Saturday as we were working six days a week. Some weeks I would drive home after work on Wednesdays so I could take Gina out to do some shopping because we only had one car. Martelle was scheduled to be born February 19 so I asked to be laid off from my job so I could be at home when Martelle was born. The place where I was working at was a three and a half hour drive to El Centro. Martelle was born on February 19, 1999. I was with Gina in the delivery room to see Martelle born. What an experience that was. Martelle had a full head of black hair. She was in perfect condition. God had blessed us with a beautiful child. A few weeks later we dedicated Martelle to the Lord at church. In May 1999 we were driving out in the country and had a car accident. We almost went into a large irrigation canal but the truck hit a guard rail on the bridge and stopped us from going into the canal. We all could have drowned that day. God had his hands upon our lives that day and blessed us with life. Gina wanted her family to see her new daughter so she took Martelle and Marcos to Peru in June of 1999. They took down lots of used clothes to give out, Spanish Bibles and aspirin.

Back in 1998 when we were still living in San Jose I bought a parcel of land there. I wasn't sure what I would do with the land at the time. When we were living in San Jose in 1998 I became aquainted with some orphan children living there. They were three brothers and two sisters. Their mother had died and their father had abandoned them. They were living in a one room dirt floor shack with no lights or running water. They cooked their food over a wood fire when they had food to eat. Gina suggested that we start taking them rice, beans and fish several times a week. When we left San Jose God gave me a burden for these children as they had no one to provide for them. We talked to Gina's grandparents to see what we could do for these kids. Gina's grandmother Mercedes said that if we would provide the money to her that she would open her house up to them everyday and that the kids could go to her house everyday for their meals and to wash their clothes and bathe. So we started sending money every month starting in 1999 to Gina's grandmother Mercedes so she could cook for these children and help us to take care of them. My parents both died when I was eleven years old. So I know how it is not to have parents and be an orphan. My heart went out to these five orphan children.

In January of 2000 we decided to build a house on the land that we had bought. Gina's grandfather Felix supervised the project and built us a five bedroom house to be used as an orphanage. When it was finished the orphans all moved into their new house. Their names were Lizbet, Dogomar, Miguel, Rodman and Doti the youngest girl. This was the beginning of a new life for these children. They had been living in a one room shack with a dirt floor all of their lives. Now they had a house with electricity, lights, and running water and two bathrooms. I was so happy for these children and I know that they were blessed. We have also been buying them new clothes, shoes and school uniforms. With the help of God we have been able to support these children eight years now. We have received some financial support from Mark Fox and his wife Gaby from Florida. We have continued to make short term trips to Peru to visit and see how the orphans are doing. The trips in 2001, 2002, and 2003 we were able to take down three cases of Spanish Bibles, five hundred toothbrushes along with six hundred pounds of good used clothes and shoes.

Gina's grandparents are our lifeline to everything that happens in Peru. We are constantly talking with them on the telephone. There are so many people that go to them and ask for our help. We have people that need financial help to get medical needs at the hospital or to get help at the clinic. Some people need help to buy new tools for their work so we buy them new tools. We have bought electrical materials for the TEC school in San Jose, and art supplies for the kindergarden school in the village of San Jose. God has used Peru to show me how much we have in the United States and how little the people have in Peru. Gad has blessed me with so many talents and wants me to use them to bless the people of Peru. Especially the gift of giving.

Chapter 14 The Cards

Finally in January 2003 Gina's and Marco's permanent residency cards arrived. They were a few years late in arriving. Now we would be able to return to Peru to live for extended periods of time. Gina and Marcos can stay outside of the United States for eleven months and two weeks straight then they have to return to the United States for a few days then they can leave again.

We have been very anxious to return to Peru but it has not been God's timing just yet. In May of 2004 while I was working at a construction project I got a very bad hernia. I had to have an operation and was off work and recuperation for six weeks. Then I returned to my job for about three weeks until I was laid off because the project was finished. We are waiting for the Lord to reveal his plans for us. This has been a blessing for me as God gave me the inspiration to start writing my biography. Also I have returned to doing research, buying and selling in the stock market. I had studied to be a stock broker back in 1993 with Baraban Securities. Our daughter Martelle has been studying ballet for the past year. She had a recital last June and is getting ready for another recital this June. Marcos was student of the month for February and is taking guitar lessons now. Last year he was student of the month five times. Martelle is also a very outstanding student in her Kindergarten class.

When I started writing this book there was very little opposition. The farther along I got the more I have encountered spiritual warfare.

Satan doesn't want this book to get written so people can hear my testimony. He has thrown so many darts at me during the time of writing this book. I think the most part of it is that this book is about my testimony of Jesus Christ.

When Jesus was here on earth he was a witness to the first twelve disciples. They got to know Jesus and were witnesses to His life and the things that He did. His disciples saw the miracles that He performed and saw him face to face daily. I have seen Jesus face to face when I was killed in the truck accident. Many times have I seen miracles done after asking Jesus to do them. People and animals were healed, and things provided by God after praying and asking. Yes God is real and alive. I bare witness to this because of my experiences with God and His Son Jesus. I was one of the most wicked and terrible sinners that walked the face of God's earth. From the marrow of my bones to the ends of the hairs on my head I was full of sin. Jesus has washed me clean of my sins and changed my heart. Jesus has been taking away the garbage out of my life. He has taken away the desire to smoke cigarettes, marijuana, heroine, cocaine, alcohol, lying, cheating sexual immorality and other undesirable things. I know that Jesus is real because He has delivered me from the bonds of sin. Only God's love and the blood of Jesus can cleanse us of our sins and create a new heart and a new person. The Holy Spirit of God who Jesus sent to us helps us with our new spiritual life. God has given me a really great metaphor for this. Every person is like a light fixture with light bulbs and cords. The problem is that there is no light coming from the light bulb. The reason why is because there is no electricity to make the light shine and be bright. The light fixture is not plugged into the power. Jesus Christ is the true power and what is missing from every persons light fixture and bulb. When we confess with our mouths that we are a sinner (Romans: Chapter ten verses nine and ten) and believe in our hearts that Jesus was raised from the dead on the third day we are born again. This is when the Holy Spirit enters into our hearts. Our light fixture cords get plugged into the power of Jesus and our light bulbs start shining with the light of God. It is also at this time that God starts cleaning up our lives by taking away the sin that was in our bones and flesh. We will not be made perfect until we get to heaven but we will be new creatures in God. Our old sin nature will be constantly fading away.

I didn't have Godly parents to teach me the ways of the Lord Jesus. So when God gave me my wife Gina and my son and daughter I was given the opportunity to start teaching them about the things of the Bible and about God and his Son Jesus. I started teaching Marcos when he was about three years old. He has been praying to God for about three years now and so has Martelle our daughter. We read the Bible quite often and I tell them Bible stories. I also tell them about my many experiences that I have had with God. They always enjoy hearing the stories I have to tell.

Chapter 15 The Learning Process

Gina and the kids will be traveling to Peru the 23 rd of July ahead of me as I am working on a remodel project of two schools in the town of Imperial which is three miles north of El Centro. I will be leaving the sixth of August and will arrive in Lima on the seventh and will meet them in San Jose on the eight of August. Gina will be taking several hundred pounds of clothes and two hundred and fifty toothbrushes. She will also be taking aspirin and arthritis medicine and toys to give out. We also purchased about thirty boxes of crayons and several dozen water color kits for the kindergarden school in San Jose. Each trip that we make to Peru is very special. The people in San Jose all know when we will be arriving and they are always excited because they know that we will be bringing many things to give out. They are especially anxious to get some clothes. What a blessing it is to be able to give to others who have very little. God has always given me an abundance of things. Every time that I give away from what God has given me He blesses me mightily. One day Gina and myself were in Pucallpa doing some things and we stopped to eat lunch at a restaurant. We got a table out on the sidewalk in front of the restaurant. As we were finishing eating a young man came close to our table. I could see that he was crippled and had no legs below his knees. He asked me if he could have what was left on my plate. I looked at him and he had such a sad look on his face. It was obvious that he was hungry. I told him that he couldn't have what was left on my plate but that I would order him a full chicken dinner and a soda if that was all right with him.

He said yes of course. So I told the waitress to bring my new friend a chicken dinner with a soda as fast as she could. When the young man saw and heard that I had ordered him a chicken dinner his face lite up very brightly. A few minutes later the waitress brought out his food and drink. The young man was so happy and thanked me. I told him that I was a Christian and the reason that I did what I did was because I had the Spirit and love of Jesus in my heart.

God has given me the village of San Jose and the people that live there as a place of ministry. We help the school with art supplies. I use my electrical skills to help people. God always opens the door for me to meet and talk to the people in Peru. The business people are always interested in what I have to say to them. God has given me an abundance of wisdom about our modern technology in the United States. I teach the Peruvian business people how to use our modern technology. God always opens the door for me to share the Gospel of Jesus Christ with these people. I spend a lot of time preaching and teaching the gospel in Peru. The people there are so eager to listen and hear the Gospel. The only things that a person knows is what they have seen and heard or what they have been taught. Jesus Christ first taught twelve disciples. He spent a lot of time with them until they had learned what they needed to learn from Jesus. Then he sent them out into the world so they could make more disciples so that the example, work and teaching of Jesus would be passed on year after year until the present day.

God has allowed me to use many spiritual gifts to bless people so they could see with their own eyes and experience Gods reality and miracles. We hope to go down to Peru next year which is 2006 to live. It is my hearts desire to work with orphans and abandoned youth.

Today is October 15 th. I have been working out at the Calvary Chapel Church property. They are building a new church on ten acres of land. My being there is by the will of God. I was asked to take over the electrical work at this project. It was a major task for me to do this. I had to evaluate what had been done and then put all of the puzzle together. I had to do some electrical designing also with the lighting. God would not allow me to do anything else because he wanted me specifically to work on this church project. What happens in our lives is by divine plan of God. God has a perfect plan for each and everyone of his children. We can choose to do things on our own but God will use these things for his plans and his Glory.

We have been going through some heavy duty financial trials for the past two years. Gina had two operations last year and I had a hernia surgery. The transmission went out in our car and we had to replace it along with new brakes, and all new steering system. I was off work for over a year with no income. I was forced to borrow twelve thousand dollars to keep us going. We are watching to see how God will get us through this major trial.

Chapter 16: Listening To God

Sometimes we can get so caught up in the circumstances and are constantly focusing on them that we lose sight of who we are in Jesus. God provided a way for me to pay back the money I had borrowed by providing a zero per cent loan on the money I had borrowed. What a blessing. He also taught me some very good lessons about money and buying things. Many people so often want to buy something that they think they need and then they buy it only to find out later that they got bored with what they had bought soon after buying the thing. God knows what things we will be content with so we should always ask him to provide what we need. Philippians 4: 19. In 1994 I made some investments without seeking guidance from God. The investments turned out bad and I lost a large amount of money. Several years later I made another large investment in the stock market. This investment went bad also. I make this investment without seeking wisdom from God also. I learned a very hard lesson about investing. What I did learn is that I would have been much better off financially if I had prayed and asked God for his direction concerning the investment of the money that he gave me.

So often we don't even seek out direction and advice from God. We are in to big of a hurry to do things and jump into something without seeking Gods counsel. Afterwards we realize that we made a big mistake and suffer and reap the consequences form our actions. Another good example of not praying about something and seeking counsel from the Bible is this. When I got married to my present wife in Peru I thought that it was the right thing to do and that she was the right person to marry. God tried to stop me but I wouldn't listen to him. It turned out to be a mistake according to Biblical principals. The person that I married was not a spirit filled born again Christian. This made me unequally yoked. I have reaped the consequences from this unequally yoked marriage. I have hundreds of stress filled days and nights because of this mistake. If I had sought out Gods counsel concerning getting married to my present wife I know that I would have made a different decision. I made a commitment to God with my marriage vows and I will stand by them.

God has taught me so many things by the power of the Holy Spirit. As a Christian that has been discipled I have experienced the reality of the need to be discipled. When a person repents and believes in Jesus Christ they are then filled with the Holy Spirit. Next a new believer needs to be nurtured and discipled as long as the believer is willing. The new believer needs to grow in Christ similar to a tree or a plant. They both need water. A tree needs regular water and fertilizer to grow. A new Christian needs spiritual water. This spiritual water is the Word of God or the Bible. Every Christian must take in spiritual water to grow strong in the Lord. Without spiritual food and water a person will not grow strong and mature as a mature Christian. Without spiritual growth there will be very little spiritual fruit. This kind of person will not be a very good witness for Jesus Christ as they will not have much of a testimony of any experiences with God.

Young Christians learn from other mature Christians. They learn by studying the Bible and by watching other Christians. We also have as a perfect example the Lord Jesus. He took twelve men and made them disciples by discipleing them. He was their example. Jesus taught them to be servants just as He was. The Bible teaches us all about Jesus and what he was all about. By studying the Bible we can learn how to be the kind of person that God wants us to be and by learning also from other mature spirit filled Christians. The Bible teaches us that the Holy Spirit teaches us also.

I know that the gift of salvation from God is very special. Why is that so? Because so many people go through life rejecting God and His Son Jesus. So many people will not concede that they are sinners. I never thought that I was a sinner for many years. Then one day God allowed me to repent and ask Jesus into my heart. I totally realized then that I was a sinner and that Jesus died for me and my sins. Next I experienced in my heart and mind the reality of God's forgiveness. It was real and I had tasted it. This Book Redeemed was inspired by my experiences with The Father, Jesus and the Holy Spirit. My testimonies are the result of my experiences with Jesus and the Holy Spirit. God Himself is my is my witness. The miracles that I have asked God to do were all done by Jesus. I was a witness to them. I am led by God to share my experiences and my testimonies with others so that others would have the desire to know the living God: The Father, Jesus, and The Holy Spirit. That others would encounter in their hearts the reality of God and salvation by the blood of Jesus.

So often when I mention hell to people their reaction is one of disbelief. So many people don't believe that hell is real and that is exist. What a lie that is.

I am no different that any other human being on this earth. Anyone can encounter salvation, redemption and eternal life in heaven by the blood of Jesus. All that is necessary is confession as a sinner and belief that Jesus died on the cross and rose on the third day. The book of Romans chapter ten verses nine and ten states this. That if thou shalt confess with thy mouth the Lord Jesus, and shalt believe in your heart that God hath raised him from the dead, your shall be saved. For with the heart man believeth unto righteousness, and with the mouth confession is made unto salvation.

Soon after my conversion with Jesus I was so happy that I had received Christ as my Lord and Savior. I would go out on my bicycle and look for people to tell them about Jesus and how I had been filled with the Holy Spirit. I had so much desire to know about Jesus and who He was that I was reading my Bible ten to twelve hours a day. I went to church on Sunday morning and again Sunday night. There was a Bible study on Thursday night that I went to also. I had a big desire to be around other Christians and to learn as much as I could about Jesus and the word of God.

The only way to learn about Jesus is by seeking him in prayer, reading the Bible, hearing the Gospel preached and taught and allowing the Holy Spirit teach you. We also learn by others who teach us what

God has taught them and by seeing the Holy Spirit in their hearts and lives. We should desire to be just like Jesus.

Chapter 18 Examples

When I was eleven years old I lost my two most precious examples in my life. They were my mother and father. A child's parents are there example for everything. Whatever a parent does the child wants to do also. If a father smokes and drinks alcohol the child will think that it is all right and want to do it also. When parents use foul language the child learns these bad words and they will become part of their vocabulary. Everything that a parent does that is bad the child will want to do because they think it is all right to do because their parents do it.

The Bible talks about parents being examples for their children. When parents live Godly Christ like lives their children will have excellent examples for how to live and act. When these children grow older they will know how they should live and how to act. Hopefully they will have accepted Jesus as their Lord and Savior. If the offspring choose to go another direction that is their choice. They have a free will. I know that after I was filled with the Holy Spirit and started growing close to Jesus that this was the most precious thing that existed in the whole world. This is to know the living God, His Son Jesus, and the Holy Spirit. I lost my parents but I was blessed with a new family. God the Father, His Son Jesus and the Holy Spirit. My heavenly Father and His Son are my examples for how to live and act with my life.

God knows everyone's heart and mind. When a person confesses to God that they are a sinner and the person believes in their heart that Jesus died for their sins they are immediately forgiven and filled with the Holy Spirit. God is then their Father. Their Heavenly Father. He is their new example as is His Son Jesus about how to act and behave. If we accept God he accepts us as one of His children. We then belong to the family of God.

I was so happy and thankful when I realized that I was a child of God. I knew perfectly clear that I had been given salvation and that my heart had been filled with the Holy Spirit. From that time on I wanted to know everything about Jesus and who he was. I wanted to be just like Him and do the same things that he does. There is nothing more important to me than my personal relationship with the living

God. Jesus who is my example takes the place of my worldly parents. I want to be just like Him in all that I do.

My daughter asked me what the meaning of fear was tonight at the dinner table. I gave her the explanation. Then I got to thinking how fearful people will be when Jesus comes back. At the white throne judgment when Jesus says depart from me and go to the lake of fire and each person realizes that there is a heaven and a hell. How much fear will they have then? I know that they will be so terrified when they know that they are on their way to hell.

God has revealed to me the existence of hell. I have seen the entrance with my very eyes and also went there in the spirit. One day while I was meditating about heaven and hell I was desirous to know what would happen to people that went to hell. So I asked God if He would take me there in the spirit to see some of the things that people experience in hell. What I saw was very frightening. I saw a man standing holding a gun. He was pointing it at another man and was asking him for his money. This man was terribly frightened and you could see on his face that he feared for his life. Then the man with the gun pulled the trigger and shot the other man. The look on his face was so gruesome as he had just been shot then fell on the ground. Then I could see inside the heart and mind of the man who had shot him. He then felt tremendous pain and sorrow because he had just killed a man. Then the scene was replayed over and over again. This man that had killed the other man kept getting tormented by the replaying of what he had done to this man by killing him. He kept experiencing the horror of what he had done over and over again. This never stopped. He will suffer the horror of his actions for ever.

Yes there is so much to fear from God. The Bible says that every knee will bow and every tongue will confess that Jesus is Lord. When Jesus returns this earth will be full of fear. People will then see that it wasn't just a story tale about Jesus. But it will be too late then. God has allowed me to see the reality of His Son Jesus and the reality of hell. I know that here is a heaven also. God has shown me many things and it is for me to share these things with the world. I have very little as to material things but what is most important of all is my testimony of Jesus Christ and the wisdom that God has given me. Jesus Christ is the

Savior of mankind and the Son of God. He created the heavens and the earth and he is the one who gives life.

Jesus started the discipleship process with the first twelve disciples. Then more were discipled. Then Jesus commanded them to go into the world and make more disciples. This process has been continued throughout the years up till the present day. When Jesus was walking by the sea of Galiliee he passed by two brothers that were fishermen. He told them to follow him and said that he would make them fishers of men. They immediately dropped what they were doing and went with Jesus. God knows everyone's heart. When God sends a Spirit filled disciple of Jesus to tell someone that they are a sinner and need to repent and believe in Jesus this is a special time. It is a day of salvation. When a person is told about salvation by the blood of Jesus and they reject it they are rejecting God and His Son Jesus. If a person hears the good news of salvation by the blood of Jesus and rejects it and then three days later they die for whatever reason they will be in hell for eternity. They rejected the invitation from God. Once you die and have gone to hell there is no changing your mind and saying now that I have experienced the reality oh hell I really would like to be in heaven. Satan just grins everytime another person arrives in hell. Don't be deceived by satan and spend eternity in hell.

I am sharing my testimony with all who will listen. Just as Jesus's disciples gave their testimonies of their experiences with Jesus I have told about my personal accounts with God. I have prayed to God and had my prayers answered. I have prayed to God for him to heal sick people and sick animals. They were healed instantly by the power of Jesus. I saw this with my own eyes. I have seen Jesus bring a dead fruit tree back to life. One day God spoke to me about smoking. He said that it was a bad witness for me to smoke. I asked God to cleanse my body from the nicotine and take away the addiction and desire to smoke. Then I told God that I would not buy anymore cigarettes and never put one in my mouth again. My faith in God that He could deliver me from smoking came true. I was delivered from smoking. I have never smoked a cigarette since asking God to deliver me from smoking. I never went through withdrawals from nicotine. These are just a few of the miracles I have seen God do. Repent and believe in Jesus. In the book of James chapter one verse five it says if any of you lack wisdom, he should ask God who gives generously to all and it will be given to you. Ask believing that God will do this. A person must believe that God will do everything that he says he will do. Everything that happens to a person is allowed by God. Ephesians chapter five verse twenty says: Giving thanks always for all things unto God and the Father in the name of our Lord Jesus Christ. If you are walking with God believing in Him and resting in His arms you are right where He wants you to be. If you are not then I know that you do not have the peace of God in your heart and in your life. Trusting in God for all things that we need is the sweetest attitude to have.

The Bible says that all things work for the good for those who love the Lord. Giving thanks for all things unto God the Father in the name of Jesus Christ. God will cause whatever that is needed to happen in your life to help you to be doing exactly what God wants you to be doing. Studying the Bible and praying will cause us to grow stronger spiritually. Individually we have to allow ourselves to be watered by God. Then God will bring forth spiritual fruit that others will see. Matthew chapter seven verses 17 thru 20 say even so every good tree bringeth forth good fruit, but a corrupt tree bringeth forth evil fruit. A good tree cannot bring forth evil fruit, neither can a corrupt tree bring forth good fruit. Every tree that bringeth not forth good fruit is hewn down and cast into the fire. Each person is likened unto a tree. Ephesians chapter five verse nine says for the fruit of the spirit is in all goodness and righteousness and truth. Ephesians chapter four verse eleven says and He gave some apostles, and some prophets, and some evangelists, and some pastors an preachers. God has given us spiritual gifts to use but so many people refuse to believe that they exist today and that they can use them. Believing is the key to the issue of using spiritual gifts.

The Bible says that if you believe that Jesus died for your sins you shall be saved. The Bible also says that God has given us spiritual gifts to use also. So use them. Jesus tells His disciples to go out into the world and preach the gospel and use the spiritual gifts. The disciples were filled with the Holy Spirit just as all born again Christians are. All spirit filled Christians have the ability to use the spiritual gifts that God has given us to use. It is because of unbelief that so many do not use these gifts or the person has been taught that they don't exist today.

Jesus told his disciples when He sent them out these instructions: Go and announce that the Kingdom of Heaven is near. Heal the sick, raise the dead, cure the lepers and cast out demons. Give freely as you have received. As born again Christians we have inherited the same things as the first disciples. All you have to do is believe this and accept it. Ephesians chapter one verses 13 and 14 say: And because of what Christ did, all you others too, who heard the Good News about how to be saved, and trusted Christ, were marked as belonging to Christ by the Holy Spirit, who long ago had been promised to all of us Christians. His presence within us is God's guarantee that He really will give us all that he promised, and the Spirit's seal upon us means that God already purchased us and that he guarantees to bring us to himself. This is just one reason for us to praise our glorious God. God has given us many things but many people refuse to accept them. People always come up with one excuse after another as to why they don't believe or use spiritual gifts. People would be truly blessed if they would just believe and do what the Bible says to do. Believe and live out what the scriptures say to do and you will be blessed. Who do you believe and honor? God or man. I have used many of the spiritual gifts because the Bible says that they are there to be used. I have seen the reality of the spiritual gifts and know that they are real and here for us to use. When I have prayed and asked God for a healing and it happens instantly I was so blessed to see it happen. How awesome it is to see a miracle happen with your own eyes. The Bible tell us to be Christ like. Therefore we can do the things that Jesus did because He says so. In 1990 when I was living in San Diego my cat Moosie had a very bad eye infection. Her eyes were swollen and pus was coming out of them. I didn't have any money to take her to the veterinarian so I laid my hands on her and prayed and asked God to heal her. He healed her instantly. There are no boundaries as what God can do. Everyday we need to give honor to God. Looking to Jesus as our guide, example, and for strength. We need to draw our wisdom from Jesus. This is being obedient to Him and honoring Him.

God calls us to worship him. But so many Christians are hindered in their lives because of idol worship. I have learned that God wants us serving Him every day of our lives. Jesus has to be more important to a Christian than anything else in this world. Early in my Christian life I felt like I was lacking a super close and intimate relationship with God on a daily basis. When I made God and the Bible the most important thing in my life I encountered God in the most intimate way. I started fasting for two and three days at a time. God honors my fasting with answers to prayers that came during and after the fast. God rewards those who honor Him by being obedient to the things that He calls us to do. A parable: If a man is cold and wants warmth he must chop and cut wood to make a fire so he can be warmed. If we want more of the things that God has for us we must do what is required to get them. To know God intimately one must seek Him in the Spirit as He is a spirit. Each person must seek God in every aspect to their life. This is an all day every day way of life. If not then you are spending to much time engulfed in the things of the world. Maybe you are constantly focused on circumstances that surround your life. The Bible says to cast our cares on Jesus. He will carry our burdens. This frees us up to focus on the Lord and to pray and worship Him. Of course we have to go to work and do our jobs, but we can still do this and worship the Lord and work for the Kingdom of God. Jesus suffered so much on His way to the cross. He died and shed his blood then sent the Holy Spirit so we could know Him intimately and personally. He did this so all people could go to heaven and live there for eternity. Don't take your salvation lightly. You will miss out on knowing the Lord and Savior the way God has intended it to be. The old saying you get out what you put in is really true with God. In the second book of Corinthians chapter nine verse six The Law of Spiritual Action and Reaction it says: But this I say, He which soweth sparingly shall reap sparingly, and he which soweth bountifully shall reap also bountifully. Are you a person that gives sparingly and prays sparingly? In the book of Colossians chapter four verses five and six it says: Make the most of your chances to tell others the Good News. Be wise in all your contact with them. Let your conversation be gracious as well as sensible, for then you will have the right answer for everyone. The Bible is kind of like a recipe book. If you use all of the ingredients and the right amounts the food that was prepared will turn out just right. A person can't pick and chose some things to do and not others with the Bible. We must use the whole Bible and all of the recipes in it. This brings us back to discipleship. A new believer needs to be discipled. He needs to learn to pray daily, He needs to learn to pray for everything. He must believe in the Person Jesus Christ and what his blood that was shed means. Discipleship will accomplish today the same as the discipleship that the first twelve disciples got when they were discipled by Jesus Christ. Being a born again Christian is a constant way of life that consist of every second of every day of your life. We must focus on Jesus at all times. For He is our source of strength, energy and faith. If you have been filled with the Holy Spirit then you know that God is real, that Jesus Christ , the Holy Spirit is real and the Bible is real. If your aren't doing what the Bible says to do why aren't you?   Not obeying Jesus and His word is the same as a disobedient child. God will do what is necessary to cause you to be obedient. But some people just keep on making there spiritual lives a disaster by not obeying the scriptures and doing what God says to do. Plain and simple just believe and do what the Bible says to do. It is not difficult if you seek God and ask Him to help you. The Bible says you have not because you ask not. If you are sincere God will honor and bless your efforts.

Repent means to turn away from. When we repent of our sins and turn away from them God immediately starts blessing our lives. Being a born again child of God can be very easy. Just believe what the Bible says. Everyone has the ability to do this. Every born again Christian should desire that all people would know Jesus as their Lord and Savior just as they do. As a born again Christian do you have this heart attitude? If so are you sowing the seed of Jesus in people's hearts? God is the one who causes a person to grow. We just plant the seed.

Sam Cannon planted the seed of Jesus in my heart. I didn't reject it but immediately believed and repented. I didn't say to myself that I would follow Jesus as soon as I stopped using drugs, stopped selling drugs, stopped abusing alcohol etc. etc. God is the one who takes the garbage out of our lives. When we set out seeking Jesus he will take away the desire in our flesh to do bad things such as drugs, alcohol, cigarettes and sins in general. When a person has experienced this Godly source of change in their life they should be busting at the seems to tell others. The Bible in Matthew chapter ten verses thirty two and thirty three: Jesus says whosoever therefore shall confess me before men, him will I confess also before my Father which is in heaven. But whosoever shall deny me before men, him will I also deny before my Father which is in heaven.

I don't preach any specific religion because a religion is not what gets a person to heaven. I preach the blood of Jesus. This is what paid the price for sin. Neither gold nor silver or any other material thing can buy passage to the Kingdom of Heaven. The book of Colossians chapter one verses twenty eight and twenty nine say: So everywhere we go we talk about Christ to all who will listen, warning them and teaching them as well as we know how. We want to be able to present each one to God, perfect because of what Christ has done for each of them. This is my work, and I can do it only because Christ's mighty energy is at work within me. What else I have within me is the Holy Spirit that shines brightly in my body. God's Holy Spirit is the one who inspires the words that come out of my mouth.

One day when I was waiting for a taxi to take me to the village of San Jose in Peru, a man that I had seen there before came up to me. It had been a few months since I had seen this person and he asked me how I was doing and where I had been. I told him that I had gone to the United States for a few months. He wanted to know what kind of work I did. I told him that I was a professional electrician in California but when I was in Peru I served the Lord as a missionary. I then asked him if he knew Jesus as his savior. He said no and then asked for more information about salvation. I started to tell him about what it said in the book of Romans about how everyone was sinner and destined to go to hell. Right after I started witnessing to this man I felt the Holy Spirit take over my vocal cords. I could hear the words coming out of my mouth but it was the Holy Spirit that was the one speaking. I didn't notice anything around me at all. Then the Holy Spirit finished speaking through me. Then my eyes were opened like normal and there were five men standing in front of me. They were all listening intently to every word that came out of my mouth. When I was speaking to the first man I didn't realize that four more had walked up also. They were drawn to me by the words that were coming out of my mouth. I was preaching salvation by Jesus Christ and his death on the cross. I told these men that they could confess their sins and believe in Jesus and receive salvation. I could see by the look on their faces that they knew what they had heard was the truth. I share my testimony with all who will listen because heaven and hell do exist. I know how hard it is to admit that you are a sinner. People don't stop to think that they really are sinners. Have you ever told a lie? Have you ever stole something? Have you ever committed adultery? Everybody is a sinner. I preach the things that God has called me to preach and I share my experiences in hopes that one or more persons will be inspired to confess to God that they are a sinner and believe in the blood of Jesus that was shed on the cross. By believing in Jesus you will be set free from the bonds of satan and your eyes will be opened. May God's grace fall upon you today that you will ask Jesus to be your Lord and Savior.

So many people talk about no life after death. I say that is a lie of the devil. I have died in a auto accident and my spirit continued to live. I was close to entering the gate of hell when Jesus intervened and stopped me before I went in. I was spared this terrible fate because of the grace of God and the love of Jesus Christ. After seeing Jesus face to face He restored life into my dead body. The odds of this happening to many people are astronomical. When I was told that I was a sinner and needed to repent and believe in Jesus I did so that same day. I say to all that I can don't let satan beguile you. There is a hell and each person who does not repent of their sins and believe that Jesus shed his blood on the cross for all the sins of the world will go to hell. When you read this book I pray that God will open up your heart so that you can take the step of faith to believe. This is your day for salvation, confess your sins to God, and call upon the Lord Jesus and be saved. Matthew chapter twenty five verses thirty one thru forty six say: 31: But when I, the Messiah, shall come in my glory, and all the angels with me, then I shall sit upon my throne of glory. 32 And all the nations shall be gathered before me. And I will separate the people as a shepherd separates the sheep from the goats, and place the sheep at my right hand, and the goats at my left. 34: Then I, the King, shall say to those at my right , Come, blessed of my Father, into the Kingdom prepared for you from the founding of the world. 35: For I was hungry and you fed me, I was thirsty and you gave me water, I was a stranger and you invited me into your homes;   36: naked and you clothed me; sick and in prison, and you visited me. 37: Then the righteous ones will reply, Sir, when did we ever see you hungry and feed you? Or thirsty and give you anything to drink? 38: Or a stranger, and help you?

Or naked, and clothe you? 39: When did we ever see you sick or in prison, and visit you? 40: And I, the King, will tell them, When you did it to these my brothers you were doing it to me! 41: Then I will turn to those on my left and say, Away with you, you cursed ones, into the eternal fire prepared for the devil and his demons. 42: For I was hungry and you wouldn't give me anything to drink; a stranger, and you refused me hospitality; naked, and you wouldn't clothe me; sick, and in prison, and you didn't visit me. 44: Then they will reply, Lord, when did we ever see you hungry or thirsty or a stranger on naked or sick or in prison, and not help you? 45: And I will answer, When you refused to help the least of these my brothers, you were refusing help to me. 46: And they shall go away into eternal punishment; but the righteous into everlasting life.

Do you wish to be a goat and be sent to hell? Take the step of faith and believe in the Blood Of Jesus!!!!!!!